TEE VEE HUMPHREY

Tee Vee Humphrey

by JOHN LEWELLEN

ILLUSTRATED BY KURT WERTH

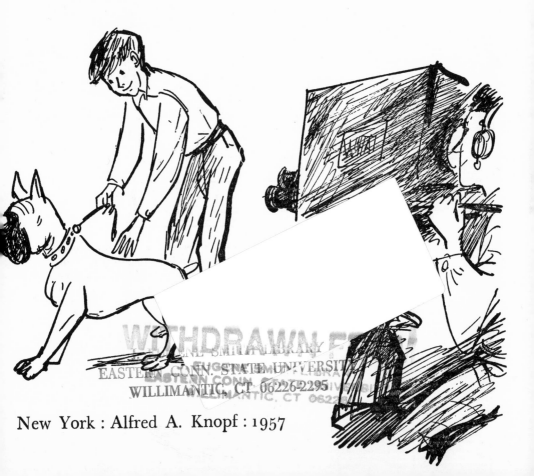

New York : Alfred A. Knopf : 1957

L. C. catalog card number: 56–5281

ⓒ WILMA LEWELLEN, 1957

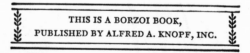

THIS IS A BORZOI BOOK,
PUBLISHED BY ALFRED A. KNOPF, INC.

To my most constant and prejudiced audience

Wilma, Lu Ann, and Tom

CONTENTS

TEE VEE HUMPHREY

HOW TEE VEE GOT HIS NAME

FROM the first time that Tee Vee Humphrey thought about what he wanted to be when he grew up, he knew exactly what he wanted to be when he grew up.

He wanted to be in television. Sometimes he wanted to be a television announcer, sometimes a great television actor, sometimes a television comedian, sometimes a television cameraman, sometimes a television director shouting orders at cameramen and actors alike.

But whatever part of it he wanted to be, and that changed from week to week, he always knew that some part of television was for him.

[3

Maybe his name had something to do with it.

Of course, his real name was Theodosius Valentinius Humphrey. But everybody quit using it when it lost a softball game on the playground at school. Young Humphrey fielded the ball and Billy Herman yelled, "Theodosius Valentinius, throw it home!" But by the time Billy could say "Theodosius Valentinius" the runner already was safe at home.

Everybody was buying TV sets about that time and Theodosius Valentinius's initials were T.V., so every-one started calling Theodosius Valentinius just plain T.V. Theodosius Valentinius himself made words out of the initials because it did not seem right for a boy so young to sign his name "T. V. Humphrey." He started signing it Tee Vee Humphrey and the name stuck.

The name caught on all the quicker because the kids in the neighborhood made a little chant of it, which they shouted together: "TEE-Vee, HUM-phrey; TEE-Vee, HUM-phrey; TEE-Vee HUM-phrey." Billy tried another version, "TEE-Vee HUM-phrey IS a SIS-sy," but Tee Vee proved him wrong about that by pinning his shoulders to the ground three times in a row. And the girls tried, "TEE-Vee HUM-phrey IS a SWEET-y." This embarrassed Tee Vee, but he remembered that

4]

a gentleman does not go around pinning little girls' shoulders to the ground. Besides, he did not really, really mind too much.

When Tee Vee was in the fifth grade he decided that if he were going to be in television it was about time he got in television. He wasn't getting any younger.

Tee Vee talked the matter of his television career over with his pal Billy Herman, and also Johnny Cox and Fred Jones. He decided that he would start out as a great television actor. Billy, Johnny, and Fred all thought this would be a good idea.

So one evening right after school he went to the local television station, WHAT. (People always said "WHAT a station!") He advised the pretty young girl at the desk in the lobby that Tee Vee Humphrey was now ready to accept a job as a great television actor.

This startled the girl somewhat. She swallowed her chewing gum.

"What did you say your name was?" she asked.

"TEE-Vee, HUM-phrey," Tee Vee replied, falling into the old chant himself.

"And you said you now are ready to accept a job as what?" she asked.

"As a great actor," Tee Vee repeated. He said it

[5

with the air of a man who is such a great actor he can afford to be patient with pretty gum-chewing girls who do not understand things the first time they hear them.

The girl was beginning to turn red in the face and seemed to be choking. Tee Vee began to worry about her, but could think of nothing to do except to walk around behind her chair, pound her on the back, and ask whether she felt better. Which he did. And she said she did feel better and added graciously, "THANK ye, TEE-Vee, HUM-phrey."

She did, in fact, seem much recovered but for a moment her face showed some sternness mixed, possibly, with a trace of annoyance.

"Listen, you . . ." she began, and what she meant to continue with was, "Listen, you, this is funny, perhaps, but you have a lot of nerve coming in here and wasting my time by announcing that you are ready to accept a job as a great actor. People become great actors by hard study and by getting lots of experience before they tackle television. You are young and preposterous, and watch that you don't stumble on your way out."

But she thought of the boss, Mr. Jules, and the hard day he had had. A big-shot network guy in New York

had been telephoning long distance to bawl him out because he would not let them have a half-hour of the station's time for a new network show. The reason he would not was that he already had that half-hour sold to a local sponsor for a local show. There were contracts and signed papers, and lawyers were threatening to sue him if he let the network have that half-hour. But the network man did not seem to care whether Mr. Jules went to jail or what, and he said "Mr. Jules, clear that time!" and hung up.

So the girl at the reception desk thought maybe it would make Mr. Jules feel better, after getting bawled out by the big shot in New York, to bawl out a little shot (our own Tee Vee Humphrey). It might make him feel like a big shot himself once more.

She rang Mr. Jules's phone and announced: "Mr. Jules, a Mr. TEE-Vee, HUM-phrey, to see you." You see, because of that chant, no one ever forgot Tee Vee's name. Mr. Jules apparently repeated it too, with a question mark after it, for the girl repeated, "That's what I said—Mr. TEE-Vee, HUM-phrey." Then there was some more talk from Mr. Jules that Tee Vee couldn't hear, but then he heard the girl say, "I know you don't know him, but he will be good for you and I am sending him in."

Tee Vee thought that it was very nice of her to say he would be good for Mr. Jules, and he followed her directions to the end of the hall and opened the last door.

It opened into a big office with dark paneled walls and thick carpeting and big leather-covered chairs. Mr. Jules was seated at a great long desk and when he heard the door open he looked up at where he expected to see Mr. Tee Vee Humphrey's face. Of course he was expecting a grown man and looked too high, so he had to look down until the look came to where Tee Vee's face really was.

He was a little startled that the girl had sent a mere boy in to take up his valuable time, but you couldn't help liking Tee Vee. Tee Vee still had his school clothes on and looked all boy and Mr. Jules was rather relieved that he didn't have to face another grownup at the end of the day.

With great dignity he came from behind his desk, shook hands with Tee Vee, said he was very glad to meet him, and led him to the big leather chair in front of his desk. He then walked around to his own big

[9

swivel chair, leaned back, put his fingers together across his chest, and said, "And now, Mr. TEE-Vee, HUM-phrey, what can I do for you?"

"I am now ready to accept a job as a great actor," said Tee Vee.

Mr. Jules smiled and Tee Vee did not quite know why. But he liked Mr. Jules. He had a good face. He looked worried but kind and Tee Vee had a great desire to help him in some way. He thought Mr. Jules might be worried because he did not have enough great actors, in which case Tee Vee already was helping him by making himself available.

But Mr. Jules said that station WHAT really did not need any more great actors at the moment.

Tee Vee said he would not mind being just a great announcer if station WHAT had all the great actors it needed for the moment.

Mr. Jules said that station WHAT also had all the great announcers it needed at the moment.

Tee Vee said that if station WHAT had all the great actors and announcers it needed for the moment, he wouldn't mind too much being just a director, shouting orders at the actors and announcers.

Mr. Jules said that station WHAT had all the directors it needed at the moment to shout orders at great actors and announcers.

After a little thought, Tee Vee decided he might have to accept a job as a cameraman and offered to do that until something better opened up.

But Mr. Jules said that station WHAT had a cameraman for every camera, and a camera pusher besides, and besides all that there were certain union rules that required that all cameramen be members of the union. Was Tee Vee a union member?

Tee Vee said that he was not and added that he would have been, probably, but he did not know about it.

Very gently, Mr. Jules started to explain to Tee Vee that there might be many things about television that Tee Vee did not know about. He told him how much training and schooling actors and announcers go through, and how many of them, even after years of work, never get a chance to prove how good they are, if they are, and sometimes they are not.

He told him how much experience television directors must have—how they must learn just about all there is to know about television—before they can become good directors. And how a cameraman can make a show better or ruin it, depending on how smart he is and how much experience he has had.

In short, Mr. Jules was very kind but he was about to escort Tee Vee to the door without giving him any job at all.

Tee Vee felt desperately disappointed. But he had listened to all that Mr. Jules had said, and Mr. Jules

12]

had said it so kindly that he believed every word he heard. It even dawned on him that he was not ready to be a great actor yet, or even an announcer, or a director, or a cameraman. It occurred to him that there might be a lot he did not know about television, even though he had been watching it every evening at home after school and everything looked so easy.

How could he learn? He could not learn it at school —not in the fifth grade. His teacher did not know much more about it than he did. His father was a fireman and knew all about fighting fires, but not about television. And his mother knew how to make wonderful peanut crunch cookies, but not all about television.

Tee Vee knew that he had to stay around that station to learn about television. But how could he do that? He had a feeling you could not just stand around. Then a thought struck him. Didn't he run errands for his mother all the time? Didn't the teacher ask him to take notes to the principal?

"Mr. Jules," Tee Vee said, "I have just decided that I am available as a television errand boy."

Mr. Jules looked up at this, and hesitated. He was thinking that Tee Vee was too young to work around a TV station and that he had older page boys who could run errands most of the time. But he had a boy

[13

himself, just Tee Vee's age, and he liked boys just that age.

"I think we could agree on a price," Tee Vee said encouragingly. All at once he wanted very much to be an errand boy at station WHAT and to work for Mr. Jules.

"In fact I would work for nothing," he added, when Mr. Jules did not say anything.

Mr. Jules was wondering what the network man in New York would think if he hired a fifth-grader to work at the station. Of course Mr. Jules could not hire him full time, what with Tee Vee's schoolwork and homework. But even if he hired Tee Vee to work on Saturdays only, conferences and board meetings would have to be held in New York. Men making hundreds of dollars a week would spend their time trying to decide whether Mr. Jules should spend three dollars a week for Tee Vee's services.

Mr. Jules had his hands deep in his pockets while he was deep in thought, and felt his own money in his pockets. Why not? He could pay Tee Vee a little something himself. And it would be nice to have the boy around after dealing with grown-ups all week. Besides, Tee Vee seemed eager and perhaps the boy really would learn something.

14]

"Mr. Humphrey," he said, "report for work next Saturday morning at 9 o'clock. Saturdays only, mind you. Don't want to interfere with your schoolwork."

"Thank you, sir!" Tee Vee shouted, and jumped from his chair. He could hardly wait to get home to tell his mother that he now was in television.

That was why he closed the door on his foot as he rushed out the door, and sprawled flat on his face in the hallway.

Tee Vee blushed when Mr. Jules came to pick him up, but Mr. Jules just smiled, and patted him on the back.

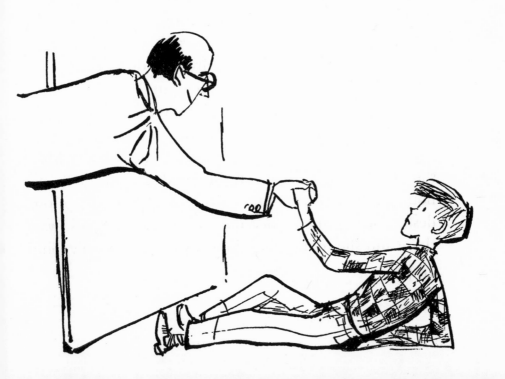

~~~~~~~~~~~~~~~~~~~~~~~~~~~~~~~~~~~~~~~

T W O

TEE VEE TRIES OUT
AS "PROP BOY"

TEE VEE asked his mother to be sure to awaken him in plenty of time Saturday morning to get ready for work. He set his alarm clock for 7. But he was so excited that he was awake and dressed long before the alarm clock rang. He was washed and scrubbed and waiting for breakfast before his mother and father were up.

After breakfast he waited as long as he could before starting for station WHAT, but still arrived half an hour early. However, the nice girl at the reception desk, whose name turned out to be Lucille Barns, was there and she took the excited young man in tow. She

16]

said Mr. Jules had left word that Tee Vee, when not running errands for other people, was to work in the "prop" department, making himself useful in any way possible. The regular "prop girl" was off on Sautrdays and Tom Betz, head of both the prop and scenery departments, needed help.

"What will I have to prop up?" Tee Vee asked. He was very confused and did not feel he was big enough to prop up anything very big. But if a *girl* could do it the rest of the week, he thought he could do it Saturdays.

"You don't have to prop up anything," Miss Barns told him. "The word 'prop' is just the word they use in television for 'properties'."

"Oh," said Tee Vee, but the way he said it convinced Miss Barns that Tee Vee knew no more than he had before about what props are.

"Properties," she continued, "as if you didn't know, are everything used in staging a show except the scenery and costumes. The furniture, the pictures, the telephones, the mirrors—all these things are props. The small props that the actors handle are called 'hand props'."

"Oh," said Tee Vee again, but this time he sounded as if he had some idea of what props were.

[17

"We keep hundreds of props in our prop rooms," Miss Barns told Tee Vee. "Mr. Betz can supply most props needed, from the ones he already has. Often, though, a show needs a prop that we do not have. Then you can go out and borrow or buy the prop somewhere else. You have to be pretty smart sometimes to find out just where you can get what's needed."

That "you have to be pretty smart" part made Tee Vee Humphrey push his chest out a little. He had expected to run errands, but apparently he also was being given a job that took brains. Mr. Jules must have a lot of confidence in him.

It was 9 o'clock now and Miss Barns led Tee Vee down the hall to the prop department, where she introduced him to Mr. Betz. Mr. Betz was a nervous little man who gave the impression that he always was being asked to do the impossible, which he often was. But he was pleasant and he greeted Tee Vee warmly.

Tee Vee's eyes nearly popped out as he caught glimpses of all the things stacked and piled in the prop room. On one shelf he saw clocks of all kinds, old-fashioned and modern telephones, a coffee grinder, table cloths, dishes, lamps, artificial flowers, and revolv-

ers. And there were many other shelves with hundreds of other items. So much furniture was stacked in the big room that one could hardly move about. Tee Vee would have liked to examine everything, but Mr. Betz had an errand for him right away.

"What was that name again, young man?" he asked.

"Tee Vee," said Tee Vee.

"That's what I thought Miss Barns said. But it's a little hard to believe the first time you hear it. Well, now, Tee Vee, I want you to go shopping at the grocery store. Kale Gompton wants a bag of groceries for his *The Animal Shop* program this afternoon. Here's some money. Get a big bag full."

"What does he like to eat?" asked Tee Vee.

"Oh, he doesn't eat the stuff," Mr. Betz said in some surprise. "He just has a monkey upset it."

It was Tee Vee's turn to look surprised.

"That show, you know, is supposed to take place in a pet shop," Mr. Betz explained. "Mr. Gompton has a very curious monkey named Sharley whom he keeps chained in the shop. When the show opens this afternoon he will pretend he has been shopping for his wife and will set the bag of groceries down on his desk. He 'accidentally' will place it just within Sharley's reach. That monkey will start investigating and

20]

before the show is over, Sharley is bound to upset the sack and spill all the groceries on the floor."

"Why would Mr. Gompton let her do that?"

"To get a laugh, of course. It always does. Makes an awful mess on the floor for the stagehands to clean up, but in television you got to get laughs. The bigger the mess, the funnier it is. So include a sack of flour in a light paper bag so it will split easily, and also a couple of dozen eggs, just loose in the big bag."

This seemed pretty silly to Tee Vee and an awful waste of groceries, especially since his mother was always talking about the high cost of food these days. But he dashed off to do as he was told. As he walked out into the hall, Mr. Betz called after him.

"Oh, yes, Tee Vee, while you're at it, you might as well pick up an empty milk bottle. We need it for a dramatic show next Saturday. This man steps out the back door to put the empty milk bottle out for the milkman, and the gangsters, hidden out there, mow him down."

That made the empty milk bottle sound mighty important to Tee Vee. But when he asked the man at the grocery store whether he carried empty milk bottles, the man said no.

Tee Vee obtained the rest of the things, although

[21

he had a little trouble making the grocer understand that he wanted the flour in a thin sack that would break easily. The man finally emptied some flour out of a good strong bag into a thin paper bag, but he obviously thought Tee Vee was crazy. After that, Tee Vee decided not to ask him to put the eggs loose in the big bag. He decided to carry the eggs back in their safe cardboard containers, *then* put them loose in the bag so they would be sure to roll out and break when the monkey spilled them. He filled the rest of the bag with inexpensive big things like boxes of breakfast cereal.

Mr. Betz was nowhere to be found when Tee Vee returned. So Tee Vee went to Miss Barns's desk and asked where he was. Miss Barns said he probably was in a conference somewhere, because in television people always are having conferences. She told Tee Vee to take it easy and not to worry until Mr. Betz returned. She also said that *The Animal Shop* program would not be on the air until 2 o'clock in the afternoon, so there was no hurry about getting the bag of groceries to Mr. Gompton.

Tee Vee returned to the prop room and carefully placed the bag of groceries on a shelf in a corner where it would not upset. He thought it might be funny to see the flour spill and the eggs break on the show, but he was certain Mr. Betz would not think it funny if the flour spilled and the eggs broke in the prop room.

There was still the matter of the milk bottle. Tee Vee decided that now was the time to use his head. It was his responsibility to get an empty milk bottle. He had no intention of failing one of his first assignments on his first day on the job. The thing to do was to get on the telephone and locate an empty milk bottle.

He opened the telephone book to the classified section and started down the list of grocery stores. To begin with, he called only stores close to the station, then those farther away. But every store he called gave him the same answer, "No, I'm sorry, but we do not carry empty milk bottles." He decided that empty milk bottles are one thing *no* grocery store carries.

Then he tried a 10-cent store, because they seem to carry everything, but they did not carry empty milk bottles either. He tried hardware stores. Same result.

In a flash of inspiration he telephoned his mother and asked whether she didn't have an empty milk bottle.

"What in the world do you want with an empty milk bottle?" his mother asked.

[23

"Well," Tee Vee replied importantly, "it's for television. You probably wouldn't understand."

"The milkman just came," his mother said, "and took all my empties."

This thing was getting serious. Mr. Betz, and Mr. Jules above him, would expect Tee Vee to be resourceful. If an empty milk bottle was needed, Tee Vee would get it. But how?

Then a thought occurred to Tee Vee that was so brilliant he felt very proud of himself. After all, who uses empty milk bottles? Why, the dairy companies do, that's who. They produce the milk or buy it from farmers and then they put it in empty bottles. They would be sure to have a supply of empty bottles on hand at all times.

Tee Vee looked in the phone book for a dairy company and made another telephone call. The very first call was successful. The man that answered the phone said sure they had plenty of empty milk bottles. No one had ever asked to buy one before, but he guessed he could sell one if Tee Vee wanted one. Tee Vee said he would be right over to get it.

This presented another problem. Tee Vee did not recognize the address in the phone book. How would he get there? Tee Vee decided to take a cab. Television

24]

was very important and that milk bottle was very important to television. A cab seemed the only sure way of finding the place and of getting back in time to deliver the groceries to Mr. Gompton. Because Tee Vee had finished filling the grocery bag with very cheap big items, he had plenty of change left to buy the milk bottle. In fact he had $2.37 left.

Tee Vee hailed a cab in front of the WHAT building and gave the cab driver the name of the dairy company. The cab driver scratched his head at first, then finally turned around and started driving. They passed Tee Vee's home and kept on going. They passed Tee Vee's school and kept on going. They reached a part of the city Tee Vee could not remember having been in before, and kept on going. They passed the city limits out into open countryside, and kept on going. Farm after farm slipped past before the dairy company's buildings came in view and the driver stopped at the front door. Tee Vee asked him to wait and went inside.

The girl at the desk quickly located the man he had talked to on the phone and the man went out back and soon returned with an empty milk bottle. When Tee Vee asked him the price, the man looked through the front door at the waiting cab and said anyone who would take a cab that far just to get an empty milk bottle, should not have to pay for the milk bottle too. He gave it to Tee Vee.

Tee Vee thought that was very nice of him. It occurred to him that Mr. Betz would consider him a very shrewd businessman to get the bottle for nothing.

At the end of the long ride back to the station, Tee Vee ran his hand into his pocket, felt the $2.37, and asked the driver how much. The driver cranked his meter and handed Tee Vee the slip. Tee Vee had not ridden in a cab before and did not know that he could have told how much the ride was costing at any point, merely by looking at the meter.

The slip read "$15.75."

Poor Tee Vee could not believe his eyes.

"There must be some mistake," he said. "This says '$15.75'."

"There is no mistake and it reads '$15.75'," replied the driver firmly. "That's a long way out there."

"But I have only $2.37," Tee Vee pleaded.

"That's too bad," said the driver. "I feel sorry for you. But I'd feel sorrier for me tonight if I turn this cab in without the money. You work here?"

"Yes."

"Then let's go see your boss."

So Tee Vee, with dragging footsteps, led the driver to the prop room. He hoped Mr. Betz was still in conference. He wasn't. He was right there. And he turned a deep purple when he heard the story. He spluttered and made funny noises as he paid the driver $15.75. The driver said something about it being customary to offer at least a small tip. So Mr. Betz turned an even deeper purple and gave the man another $1.50. Then without another word he took Tee Vee by

the shoulder and led him down the hall, past Miss Barns, and on down the hall the other way, to Mr. Jules's office.

"This boy *you* hired," he blurted out to Mr. Jules, "this boy just paid $17.25 for an empty milk bottle!"

"He *what?*" said Mr. Jules, suddenly sitting straight up in the big chair behind his big desk.

"Yes, sir," Mr. Betz continued. "We needed an empty milk bottle for that gangster show and I asked this boy to get one. He took a cab to get it, and I don't know what kind of a pleasure ride he took to get it, but the cab bill, *including* tip, was $17.25!"

"What happened, Tee Vee?" Mr. Jules asked.

Close to tears, Tee Vee explained it all to Mr. Jules.

Mr. Jules listened with stern face. When Tee Vee had finished, Mr. Jules said: "That was a serious mistake, Tee Vee. We have to watch costs around here. You have no idea how that expense item will throw the auditing department. I'll probably hear from New York about it. You meant no harm, of course. You were trying to make good on your new job. *But next time check with Mr. Betz before you run up any big bills around here!*"

Then Mr. Jules' face relaxed into a smile.

"And next time you need an empty milk bottle, Tee Vee," he said, "run over to the grocery and buy a full bottle. If you can't drink the milk, pour it down the sink. That will leave you with an *empty* milk bottle. And will cost about 30 cents, not $17.25!"

DEAD MEN DON'T
LIE (DOWN)

MR. BETZ forgave Tee Vee, after Mr. Jules did. In fact he felt a little guilty about becoming *quite* so angry, since it was Tee Vee's first day at work and everything was strange to him. He took Tee Vee to lunch at noon, and suggested he spend the afternoon getting familiar with things around the station.

He told Tee Vee that when he took the bag of groceries to Mr. Gompton he could stay around until the program was over, and learn what he could. Then he was to deliver the now-hated milk bottle to another studio, where the gangster play for the following week was to be rehearsed at 3 o'clock.

Right after lunch Tee Vee took the bag of groceries to Studio B, where *The Animal Shop* was presented. He met Mr. Gompton, who played the part of the shop's owner. What was even pleasanter, he also met Mr. Gompton's daughter, Fay, who was the same age as Tee Vee, and quite pretty. She appeared on the show each Saturday with her father.

Stagehands were setting up the last of the scenery and Tee Vee was surprised to find that the walls were made of canvas stretched on wooden frames. The canvas was painted so cleverly it looked, on camera, like solid wood and plaster. But there were real shelves and counters in the "store." And there were real birds and animals all around the place. They were rented each week from a real pet shop.

Mr. Gompton usually had three guests on his program each week. These people brought in their pets and talked with Fay and Mr. Gompton about them. After the first guest to arrive that afternoon turned the wrong way down the hall and led her pet donkey into Mr. Jules's office, Mr. Gompton asked Tee Vee to meet the others at the elevator and lead them to the right place. After all had arrived, Tee Vee helped keep the cats and dogs apart, petted the donkey when he became noisy, and made himself quite useful in other ways.

This made a good impression on Mr. Gompton, and Tee Vee was allowed to watch the program itself from the control room, a rare and exciting privilege. He wondered how the director, Mr. Berry, could keep track of what was going on. Three cameras were used on the show. Mr. Berry had three pictures, one from each camera, in front of him all the time. He had to tell the cameramen (who listened to him over ear-

phones) what shots he wanted taken, then decide which one of the three pictures he wanted to put on the air at any particular moment.

An assistant pushed the buttons that switched the pictures to the air when Mr. Berry told him to.

In addition, Mr. Berry talked frequently to the sound man, whenever the voices of Mr. Gompton and his guests sounded too loud or too soft, or whenever a movable microphone caused a shadow across someone's face. Over a loudspeaker in the control room, a man in "master control" on another floor shouted at Mr. Berry whenever he thought anything was wrong with the picture or sound. A man in still another room, the projection room where slides used on the opening and close of the show were put on the air, also talked over the loudspeaker several times. During the show he checked with Mr. Berry on whether he had the slides in the right order.

Mr. Berry also kept talking to his "floor manager," who listened through earphones. The floor manager alerted guests when it was about time for them to appear with their pets, signaled Mr. Gompton when he had used as much time as he should with a particular guest and otherwise acted as Mr. Berry's assistant out on the floor of the studio.

There was so much noise in the soundproof control room and so much was going on, so many people talking at once and so many things to watch, that Tee Vee thought he never, never could learn enough to be a great director. Or even a poor director.

But it was all very exciting. When Sharley, the monkey, crept over to the desk and started investigating the big bag of groceries, while Mr. Gompton was several feet away talking to a guest, Tee Vee started chuckling in anticipation. When the monkey finally upset the bag, and the flour and eggs crashed to the floor, he laughed out loud. It was a lot funnier than he thought it would be. Mr. Berry and everyone else in the control room laughed too, even though they had seen it happen often before. Mr. Gompton pulled the same gag about once a month and each time he rushed over and scolded Sharley just as if he had not planned it all to start with.

Tee Vee almost felt like a great comedian himself. After all, it was he who had bought the bag of groceries and had insisted that the grocer put the flour in a thin bag so it would be sure to burst.

He wanted to stay around after the show was over, but he remembered the milk bottle. He returned to the prop room, then took the bottle to Studio B in plenty of time for the gangster show rehearsal. This was a "dry rehearsal" for the following Saturday's show. It was done without cameras or even scenery. Only small hand props were used, but when an actor opened an imaginary door and stepped out with Tee Vee's super-expensive empty milk bottle, Tee Vee again felt himself getting excited. The gangsters sprang from imaginary bushes and went "tat-tat-tat-tat-tat" like machine guns. The actor stumbled forward, supposedly dead. Tee Vee was afraid he might break the bottle in falling, but he didn't. And, apparently, none of the imaginary bullets hit the bottle.

Tee Vee made a mental note to ask Mr. Betz whether he could watch the scene the following Saturday. He wanted to see it with all the scenery, costumes, music, and sound effects. All in all, the day, despite its bad start with the milk-bottle purchase, had been very enjoyable. Tee Vee went home that night with exciting stories to tell his mother and father and his pals, Billy Herman, Johnny Cox, and Fred Jones.

Mother and Father were very enthused over Tee Vee's account and told him not to worry too much about the cab fare, just to use his head a little more next time. But Billy, Johnny, and Fred were less satisfying.

[35

"You got your acting job yet?" Billy demanded, when the three boys dropped by after the evening meal.

"That takes time," Tee Vee replied defensively.

"You a director then?" Johnny asked.

"I don't think I'll ever know enough to be a director," Tee Vee admitted.

"Announcer?" Fred put in.

"No."

"What are you then?" Billy wanted to know. "When we all decided you ought to go into television, we didn't mean for you to be an errand boy all your life."

"Yeah, you been working all day, and where did you get?" Johnny interjected. "You don't mean you've been an errand boy all day and didn't get a promotion yet!"

Tee Vee remembered what he had told Miss Barns and Mr. Jules the day he applied for the job. His friends were still talking the same way. They did not know how very, very much there was to learn about television before anyone could get any of those jobs. He was very happy to have a job of any kind at the station, and hoped he could do well enough to keep it

36]

until he could learn more. But his pride was at stake. He had talked too much about all the big things he would become.

"Just you wait," he shouted. "I'm going to be on camera next Saturday!"

"Yeah, on what show?" Fred asked, with disbelief.

Tee Vee searched his mind. He wanted it to sound exciting.

"On a gangster dramatic show, that's what show," he shouted back. "Next Saturday on WHAT at 3 o'clock!"

Afterwards, of course, Tee Vee wondered why he had said that, and wished he hadn't. After that milk-bottle episode, he was lucky he still had any job at all.

He spent a bad week, Tee Vee did. What would his friends think when they watched that show and he was not on it? He tossed in bed at night and worried by day.

Of course Tee Vee had no way of knowing until later that the author of the gangster play was having a bad week too. Mr. Jules finally had read the script and he did not like it. Mr. Berry read the script and he did not like it either. Mr. Betz said he did not like it either, and Miss Barns said she was not really an expert but she did not like it either. So the author had to start to work all over again and there was one conference after another. The actors had to learn new speeches and then forget those and learn newer ones when the play was changed again after another conference.

Thus it was that when Tee Vee reported for work the following Saturday morning, Mr. Betz said: "The gangster play has been changed."

"Don't they need the milk bottle?" Tee Vee asked.

"Yes, they still need the milk bottle," Mr. Betz said. "But the scene has been changed a little. And instead of a bunch of gangsters, there will be one teen-age hood, a neighborhood tough. Yesterday, it was going to be a gang of hoods, but that would cost too much for actors, so they cut the gang down to one. Then, instead of the man who comes out with the milk bottle coming out the back door, he comes out the front door. And instead of getting killed, he isn't touched at all. The tough kid shoots at him, but he doesn't hit him. He is a very poor shot. Instead of hitting the man, who really is a crook, he hits an innocent passer-by. Just an innocent boy, walking by. This makes the play much sadder, and points out what a horrible thing this hood is doing in having a gun at all."

"That is very sad," said Tee Vee. "I feel sorry for that kid just walking by."

"Of course you do," said Mr. Betz. "But don't feel too sorry—not so sorry you cry. You are dead when you fall down, and dead people don't cry."

Tee Vee lost track of Mr. Betz's meaning at about that point.

"Did you say when *I* fall down?" he asked. "I thought you said something about me falling down dead."

"That's right. This last change was not made until late last night, and we have no one to play the passer-by. He is supposed to be just your age. And as Mr. Berry pointed out, we do not really need an actor. After all the passer-by does not say anything. He just walks along, natural-like, gets shot, and falls down. That's all there is to it. Anybody could do it, so you could do it. Besides, as Mr. Jules pointed out, if you are in there falling down in front of a camera, we will know you are not out buying milk bottles for $17.25 each."

So Tee Vee, through no effort on his own part, *was* going to be on camera that day, just as he had said he would be. Thinking of Billy, Johnny, and Fred, he sighed with great relief. A great load dropped from his mind.

At the dress rehearsal with cameras, he at first did not pass by at the right time, but the floor manager solved that. When Tee Vee failed to get his cue, the floor manager just gave him a shove in the back. Tee Vee did not fall right the first few times he tried it, but Mr. Berry showed him just how he would fall if he had been shot.

The scene was tried over and over again. No sooner had Tee Vee fallen than Mr. Berry would say: "All right, all right, get up. Let's try it again. And this time, Tee Vee, don't walk so fast as you pass by, and when you fall, don't throw your arms out as if you were trying to catch an eight-foot basketball."

Finally everybody was satisfied with the scene, but it took so long that the rest of the play did not get all the rehearsal time it should have had on camera.

As they went on the air Mr. Berry said: "Well, the rest of the play may be nothing, but that one scene should make people sit up and take notice."

It did.

The scene came just before a commercial. Mr. Berry needed all three of his cameras to show the passer-by approaching, the man bringing out the milk bottle and the young tough with the gun. But he also needed two of the three cameras to shoot the commercial that followed immediately. That meant that he had to keep one camera on one shot long enough to give the other two cameramen time enough to swing their cameras around to the commercial set. That was no great problem. Mr. Berry had done it many times. He needed only a few seconds to get two of the cameras into the proper position for the commercial.

But the commercials had been rehearsed separately from the play. Mr. Berry knew his problem, but Tee Vee did not.

He came onstage at just the right time, he walked

slowly enough to appear to be a casual passer-by. The tough boy took sight down his gun barrel and pulled the trigger on a blank shell. Tee Vee pretended he was shot. He clasped both hands to his stomach instead of throwing them far and wide, and he crumpled to the ground (which was a roll of green paper grass spread over the hard floor) just as Mr. Berry had told him to do. Up to that point he did everything just right.

Mr. Berry told Number 1 cameraman to hold his shot of Tee Vee lying dead on the ground, and told Cameramen 2 and 3 to swing their cameras around as fast as they could to the commercial set. Mr. Berry would have held that Number 1 camera shot of the dead boy for several seconds anyway. It was dramatic. It drove home what a terrible thing the tough boy with the gun had done.

Alas, Tee Vee at rehearsal had been told each time he fell down to jump up and try it again. He knew now, of course, that he would not be asked to try it again, but he was accustomed to getting up quickly. He had been killed. He had fallen. His job was done and done well. He jumped up and walked off-stage, brushing the dust from the seat of his pants as he did so.

And that, of course, is just what Billy, Johnny, and Fred and his parents and several hundred thousand other viewers saw on their screens at home. They saw the supposedly dead Tee Vee, get up, healthy as could be, and walk off, dusting the seat of his pants.

Tee Vee did not know what had happened until afterward. He wondered why everyone was so excited. When he found out why, he was sorry he had been on the show at all.

Billy, Johnny, and Fred made him feel no better when he saw them that night.

"I've heard," said Billy, "that the dead don't lie. But I thought that meant they don't tell a lie. I guess it means they just won't lie down and stay there."

"Anyway," said Johnny, "even if you had stayed down, you did not fall right. You didn't throw your arms out."

"And besides," Fred concluded the matter for the unhappy Tee Vee, "even if you had fallen right and even if you had stayed down, that still was not acting. You didn't say anything. Actors say things."

Mr. and Mrs. Humphrey heard sounds that almost seemed like sobs coming from Tee Vee's bedroom that night. They stood in front of the door and said rather

[43

loudly to each other that they did not think it was Tee Vee's fault at all. The cameraman or the director or somebody must have made a mistake.

Tee Vee overheard, as he was meant to, and he did not really believe it, but he dropped off to sleep.

TEE VEE BECOMES A TALKING ACTOR

REGARDLESS of what Tee Vee's schoolmates thought, Mr. Jules did not blame Tee Vee for what had happened when he was shot. No one had told him to lie still on the floor until the floor manager signaled him to get up. Tee Vee was new at the station, Mr. Jules pointed out, and Mr. Berry should have instructed him about such things. Mr. Berry just had not thought about it.

So Tee Vee kept his job. During the following weeks he learned his way around the station and what the many departments did. He learned the names of all the people. When he was not busy working for Mr.

Betz in the prop department, he made himself useful wherever he could. He soon became just about the best errand boy any station ever had.

Of course he had to take a lot of kidding from Billy, Johnny, and Fred about not being an actor yet, but finally his big break did come.

It was one of those things that surprisingly happens very frequently. Tee Vee became an actor because he was in the right place at the right time.

Sometimes it is very difficult to know when the right time is going to be, but Tee Vee got in the right *place* the day he got the job as an errand boy at WHAT. When the right *time* came along, he already was in the right place.

Tee Vee was delivering another bag of groceries to Mr. Gompton. (Mr. Gompton had decided that enough time had passed so that he could pull the monkey-flour-egg gag again.) Mr. Berry called Mr. Gompton to answer the telephone in the control room. There was a phone on Mr. Gompton's desk on *The Animal Shop* set, but this was a "dummy phone," not really hooked up to anything.

When Mr. Gompton came back from the control room, he was all excited.

"That was my wife," he shouted. "Fay just came

46]

down with the measles and it's only an hour before show time!"

"You'll have to do the show without your daughter," Mr. Berry said.

"No, the public likes to see kids on this show," Mr. Gompton protested. "I sometimes hate to admit it, but Fay is more important on this program than I am."

"Then get one of your daughter's friends to come down and take her place."

"They live too far out. They never could make it today. Besides, they don't know the show as well as Fay does. I need someone . . ."

Mr. Gompton's eye fell on Tee Vee . . . You see, Tee Vee was standing in the right place at the right time.

"Hey, Tee Vee," Gompton called. "You've been running errands and helping out around this show long enough. You know the routine. How about *you* taking Fay's place on the show today?"

"Yes, *sir,* Mr. Gompton," he accepted immediately. "And I'll do my best, sir."

A talking actor at last! That would take care of Fred Jones and the other kids. This was what Tee Vee had wanted in the first place—to be a great actor. Of course this was not quite acting like they do in the movies. Gompton and Fay used no script. They did the commercials for *Dogs Love It* dog food, the show's sponsor, from memory. The rest of the time they just talked to the guests, handled the animals, and between times made up small talk about the animals and school and home. There was no problem filling up the time. Tee Vee had noticed that any time Mr. Gompton and Fay got a dog owner or a cat owner or a monkey owner or a bird owner or even a skunk owner to start talking about his pet, he would talk all afternoon if they let him.

When Fay was on the show she followed her father around, talked to the guests too, reminded him of their names if he forgot and helped feed the animals. When it was time for the show to be over, the sound effects man rang the dummy telephone on Gompton's desk. Fay answered it, talked to herself a moment, and then announced to her father that mother had called to say they were having an early dinner and to hurry home.

So, you see, Tee Vee's job was not really as a replacement for a great actor. On the other hand, if being on television and *pretending* you are visiting a pet shop isn't acting, what is? Tee Vee was very happy to be achieving his ambition so early in his television career.

48]

He did not really count his one appearance on the dramatic show, when he was shot, because he wanted to forget that altogether.

"Don't worry about a thing," Gompton told Tee Vee. "Just do the way Fay does and you'll be okay. There's one thing you want to be sure to do just right, though. During the first commercial, while I talk about *Dogs Love It* dog food, you know Fay always feeds some to my own dog, Wooster. I want you to do the same thing. The camera will be on you and the dog while I talk about it, and we'll use a close shot of the dog gobbling up the food real hungrylike, to show how good *Dogs Love It* is. I had a time training that dog-gone dog to like the stuff, but he eats it okay now."

"The point is, you have to put the pan of dog food down in just the right place, with the dog facing the right way, so the camera can get a good close-up. Come over here. I'll put a circle on the floor with a piece of chalk so you'll know just where to put the pan, and be sure the dog is headed that way—toward Number 2 camera. Now just remember that and we'll be okay."

Whereupon Mr. Gompton left Tee Vee to do his remembering while he went over behind the set to talk to his guests and explain to them what they were supposed to do.

Tee Vee was a little worried about being on the commercial. He had been around long enough to know how important sponsors are. He knew that a show had to have a sponsor to pay the bills and that sponsors can cancel the show if there is something about it they don't like or if it isn't selling the sponsor's product. He also knew that sponsors, unlike other kinds of people, are more interested in the commercials than in the rest of the show. Tee Vee was going to have the important part in the first commercial and he wanted the sponsor to like it.

Mr. Gompton did not bother with rehearsals. He felt rehearsals would make the show seem less natural. Also, the sponsor paid so little for the show there was no money for more than enough camera rehearsal to make sure the cameras were working. But there was no reason Tee Vee could not rehearse his part in the commercial on his own, without cameras. That's what he did.

While Mr. Gompton still was out of sight behind the set talking to his guests, Tee Vee called "Wooster" and the dog came running. The dog was named

50]

Wooster," Mr. Gompton had explained, because his former owner was a man named Dr. Shire and he liked to call his dog "Woostershire." Tee Vee long since had become friendly with the dog, so there was no trouble there.

Tee Vee emptied a couple of cans of *Dogs Love It* dog food into Wooster's pan. He had no trouble finding a couple of cans of *Dogs Love It*. The cans were stacked all over the shelves, all over the counter, on the floor in front of the counter, and on the floor on both sides of the door. The sponsor wanted to be sure that no matter where a cameraman pointed his camera there would be cans of *Dogs Love It* in the picture.

Carrying the pan of dog food, Tee Vee stepped to the chalked circle on the floor. The dog, a beautiful big boxer, followed, wagging his tail in eager anticipation. Remembering his instructions, Tee Vee pushed Wooster's back end around until the dog was facing exactly toward Camera 2.

Then he started to lean over to set the pan of food down in the circle. Tee Vee certainly was not vain, but it did occur to him—would he look better on television bending over from the waist, or would that look too stiff? Maybe he would look better if he kept his back

[51

straight and gracefully bent his knees into a squatting position, and *then* placed the pan on the floor. He worried about this just in case his friends and parents might be watching their TV sets, and he thought they would be, because he had telephoned them all.

He was practicing bending and squatting when the impatient and hungry dog jumped for the pan. He hit Tee Vee on the left shoulder with his huge paws and 70 pounds of weight and Tee Vee went sprawling. The pan spilled and the *Dogs Love It* dog food was spread all over.

Well, it was a little embarrassing to Tee Vee to be lying flat on the floor, with *Dogs Love It* all around

him, and Wooster gobbling up the dog food just as it lay. On the other hand, it was good to have Wooster so eagerly cleaning up the mess. No one came running, so the accident apparently had made not too much noise and no one had noticed. The cameramen and the rest of the crew had not shown up yet, and Mr. Gompton and the guests were out of sight in back of the set.

Tee Vee was not dishonest. He had no wish to hide from Mr. Gompton the fact that he had permitted the dog to knock him over and spill dog food all over the stage. But again, if Mr. Gompton did not know about it and did not ask him about it, there seemed little point in worrying him about it. Tee Vee *was* afraid that poor Mr. Gompton might worry, because he might get to imagining what it would have been like if the accident had happened on the show itself. This almost certainly would have distressed the sponsor, and that would have distressed Mr. Gompton, who might lose his job, and Mr. Jules, who would lose the sale of the time.

While Tee Vee thought these thoughts Wooster finished removing the evidence by eagerly lapping up all the spilled dog food. He cleaned the floor quickly and to perfection.

[53

Tee Vee really did not blame Wooster for what had happened. Wooster was hungry. Mr. Gompton always cut down on Wooster's food for two days before the show. This was so the dog would be so hungry he would go after that *Dogs Love It* dog food with enough enthusiasm to satisfy the sponsor. Who could blame Wooster for getting impatient while Tee Vee practiced to find out how to look his best, bending over or squatting? Tee Vee told himself he should have reached out a restraining hand and held Wooster by the collar until the pan was properly placed in the circle.

Obviously this was something that needed more rehearsal. So Tee Vee emptied a couple more cans of *Dogs Love It* dog food into the pan, took his position once more in front of the circle, summoned Wooster, placed him back, and started a graceful swoop into a squatting position to set the pan down.

As Tee Vee at that instant discovered, Mr. Gompton had drawn the circle just a shade too close to Sharley, the monkey. She was a squirrel monkey, with a tail almost as long as a man's arm but a body hardly larger than a kitten's. Because she was so small, she hated any animal bigger than herself. And she hated Wooster most of all because he not only was big but also the star of the show. When Tee Vee pulled back on Wooster's collar, he brought the dog's tail just within reach of Sharley, straining at her chain.

You know what happened. Sharley grabbed Wooster's short tail and sank her tiny but sharp little teeth into it.

Wooster let out a horrible yowl and gave a lunge to get away, pulling Tee Vee with him, while Sharley

screamed and danced in glee. The pan of *Dogs Love It* was knocked from Tee Vee's hand and landed upside down on the floor.

"What's wrong out there?" Mr. Gompton shouted.

"Everything's fine," Tee Vee shouted back. "Wooster . . ." Then he lowered his voice so much that Mr. Gompton could not be sure just what he was saying, and then ended up good and strong, "So everything is just fine."

Mr. Gompton let it go at that, and Tee Vee wasn't much worried. After all, he knew that Wooster would clean up the mess of the spilled *Dogs Love It* dog food, as soon as he recovered from the pain inflicted by Sharley, a matter that took about 3½ seconds. And, while Wooster was cleaning up the mess, Tee Vee took steps to make sure that Sharley could not cause this trouble again on the show itself. He unsnapped her chain and refastened it a couple of feet farther away. Now, no matter how she tried, she could not possibly reach Wooster's tail while he was showing the sponsor how much he liked *Dogs Love It* dog food.

There was no more time for Tee Vee to rehearse with Wooster. The cameramen arrived and started testing their cameras. The bright set lighting came on.

The director arrived and talked with the floor manager about the order of events on the show. Mr. Gompton finished talking with his guests and came out on the set. Little more than a minute remained before the show went on the air.

While they stood on the set waiting for the opening music and the slides announcing the title and sponsor of the show, Mr. Gompton remembered one other thing to warn Tee Vee about.

"When I set the bag of groceries on the desk," he whispered, "be sure you don't move it. You might get it beyond Sharley's reach and spoil the joke."

Tee Vee promised he would not even touch the bag.

The music had started and the opening cards were on the screen. Mr. Gompton could see this on a TV screen, called a monitor, at one side of the stage. He led Tee Vee outside the door, then at just the right time, when he saw in the monitor that Mr. Berry had a shot of the door from the inside, he and Tee Vee opened the door and walked inside.

Tee Vee Humphrey was on camera! And not just to get killed while passing by either. He was an actor and he would talk for half an hour! Success, at age 11!

[57

And nothing, Tee Vee was telling himself, could go wrong with the commercial—not after all that rehearsal.

But, of course, the show was just starting. It wasn't over.

DOGS LOVE IT

PRETENDING that they had just come in from the street, Mr. Gompton and Tee Vee hung up their coats and Mr. Gompton set the bag of groceries on the desk. He appeared to do this carelessly, but actually he was very careful to set the bag exactly where he always had placed it before, so that Sharley "accidentally" could reach it.

Mr. Gompton sat at his desk and told Tee Vee he was glad he had been able to come to help out, since his daughter Fay had the measles, and told him about some of the pets his guests would bring in that day.

[59

This was a "teaser" to suggest to viewers that if they did not like what they were seeing then, they should not tune off the program because something interesting might happen later.

"Oh," Tee Vee said, each time Mr. Gompton said something.

This was not all Tee Vee had planned to say, but somehow he could not think of anything more to say. Fay always seemed to have plenty to say when she talked with her father on the show. Tee Vee had pictured himself chatting gaily and knowingly. He had imagined his friends and all the strangers viewing the show, and he could hear them saying, "My, that new boy on the program certainly is a natural, isn't he? Just listen to that voice! He certainly will be a great actor. And he sounds so intelligent, too."

That was what Tee Vee imagined, but once he *really* was in front of those cameras something happened to him. He was plain scared. What was he scared of? He didn't know. People sometimes get scared when they stand in front of a crowd to make a speech, even if everyone in the crowd is a personal friend. There was no real crowd in the studio, but there were microphones carrying the sounds to thousands of unseen people, and that was worse.

Also, a red light on the front of the camera came on every time the director decided to use that particular camera's picture on the air. The red light seemed to stare right at Tee Vee and it numbed his wits. He felt that rays from the red light had shriveled up his brain until there was nothing left.

He didn't really know what Mr. Gompton was saying, but every time Mr. Gompton's voice paused, Tee Vee said "Oh."

The "Oh" didn't sound right even to Tee Vee. It sounded like someone else's voice—someone with a very weak and colorless voice. He tried to make an "Oh" come out with some force, but that only added a kind of squeaky tone to the weak sound.

Tee Vee had never been more uncomfortable in his life. He wished desperately the half-hour were over, but he knew this half-hour would seem to keep going on and on and not stop the way half-hours at school stop.

Soon the bell announced that the first guest had stepped through the door.

"Come on, Tee Vee," Mr. Gompton said genially, but in his dazed state Tee Vee did not quite understand, so Mr. Gompton took him by the hand and pulled him along to meet the guest.

"Tee Vee," Mr. Gompton said cheerfully, "meet Mrs. Powers."

"Oh," said Tee Vee.

"Mrs. Powers has been nice enough to bring her pet parakeet in for us to see, or rather to hear, because this little fellow is one of the best talkers in the country."

"Oh," said Tee Vee.

"What's the little fellow's name, Mrs. Powers?" Mr. Gompton asked his guest.

"Say your name for the man, honey," Mrs. Powers commanded the bird in such gushy tones Mr. Gompton momentarily thought of pushing her in the face.

The bird was silent.

"Martha, Martha, Martha, Martha, Martha, Martha, Martha, Martha, Martha, Martha," Mrs. Powers cooed, trying to give the bird a small hint as to what her name was, but Martha did not take the hint. She just looked around the studio at the cameras and bright lights and acted as if she were deaf as well as dumb.

"Come on honey," Mrs. Powers pleaded, lifting the little bird's beak to her mouth and giving her a loving kiss. "Come on, honey. Say 'Martha.' Say 'Mar-tha, Mar-tha, Martha, Martha, Martha, Martha.'"

Mrs. Powers was becoming rather exasperated be-

62]

cause the bird clammed up like a gangster on the witness stand.

Mr. Gompton tried to come to her rescue, and the rescue of his program.

"Ha, ha," he laughed loudly. "So the little fellow's name is Martha. I might have known that. When it comes to parakeets, the women sure can't keep up with the men. Ha, ha! But when it comes to wives, it's sure the other way 'round. Ha, ha! Yes, sir, Ha, ha! Yes, sir, I wish some women I know were as quiet as that parakeet of yours. Yes, sir, I sure wish they were."

Mr. Gompton was gently trying to crowd Mrs. Powers toward the door, but Mrs. Powers had no intention of leaving yet. She knew that Martha talked her head off at home, and she was determined to prove to Mr. Gompton and the television audience that Martha was not as dumb as she now was acting.

"You say something to her," she instructed Tee Vee.

"Oh," said Tee Vee.

The bird said nothing.

"Say 'Hooray, the Fourth of July,' honey," Mrs. Powers tried again, and then she tried and tried again. *If at first you don't succeed, try, try again* did not seem to work with parakeets.

64]

Mr. Gompton was hoping Sharley would hurry with that bag of groceries. If the little monkey would just break all those eggs over there and spill the flour and cause a big noise, he could save the day—or at least the program. He saw that Number 1 camera was trained on the bag of groceries so that the director could switch to that picture as soon as Sharley started her investigation. The cameraman had been tipped off in advance to watch for the shot. Mr. Gompton did not want to turn around to look at Sharley for that would make it obvious that he was expecting the gag.

Tee Vee didn't think that far ahead. He wasn't thinking at all. He did turn around to look at Sharley. And then the numb feeling was blasted away by a feeling of absolute horror.

He didn't even hear when Mrs. Powers asked him to say 'Hooray, the Fourth of July' to Martha.

His eyes were on Sharley, the inquisitive monkey. The monkey was inquisitive all right and was straining at her chain. But the chain held her back at least a full foot from the tempting bag.

And Tee Vee knew why. He had moved the chain to keep Sharley from biting the dog. He thought of walking to the desk and shoving the groceries closer to Sharley so she could reach them, but if a camera

[65

caught him in the act, that would look mighty silly. And besides, he had promised Mr. Gompton he would not move the bag.

So Tee Vee just stood there, frozen to the spot, and wondered how angry Mr. Gompton would be when he discovered why his gag did not work when so sorely needed.

At that instant Tee Vee got another surprise. Suddenly the studio was flooded with parakeet talk! Apparently Martha had decided to talk . . . and talk and talk.

"Four score and seven years ago," came the clear parakeet voice. "Love me, huh? Well, by jove. Come on get up, come on get up. Parakeets can talk. Parakeets can talk. Four score and seven years ago. Four score and seven years ago." Sometimes parakeets don't make too much sense, even when they do decide to talk.

But when Tee Vee looked at Mr. Gompton's face, expecting to see great relief there, all he saw was surprise. And Mrs. Powers was so startled her hand shook so badly that Martha had trouble hanging on.

And Martha herself obviously was not talking. Tee Vee was close enough to see the beak and throat and there was no movement there.

66]

What had happened gradually dawned on Mr. Gompton and he started commenting on what a wonderful little talker Mrs. Powers had in Martha.

What had happened was that the director of the show, realizing that Martha was never going to talk during that half-hour, and that Mrs. Powers was determined to stay until she did, decided to give the bird a little electronic help. He hurriedly ordered the sound man to look up a talking parakeet recording.

The recording was slapped on the phonograph (turntable, they call them in television) in the control room. The audio engineer channeled the sound into the loud-speaker in the studio, one usually used for shows with audiences, so that the audience could hear better. Meantime the director ordered his cameramen to take no close shots of the bird. From a distance no viewer could tell that Martha was not using her own beak and throat for speaking purposes. In fact, from a distance, viewers couldn't see Martha at all.

"That was wonderful, Mrs. Powers," Mr. Gompton was saying as he pushed Mrs. Powers toward the door. "It was so nice of you to let us hear Martha talk. Do bring her back sometime, won't you. Good-bye, good-bye."

By that time he had her out the door.

[67

Some viewers may have wondered how they still could hear Martha talking so loudly and clearly after the door was closed, because the audio engineer was a little slow in cutting off the loud-speaker. For a few seconds one could hear Martha talking just as well when she wasn't there as when she was.

This show was getting to be nerve-racking and Mr. Gompton was anxious to get on to something else.

"Now Tee Vee," he said, giving Tee Vee a little shove to make sure he was awake, "you give Wooster some of that delicious *Dogs Love It* dog food while I talk to the folks a little while."

Tee Vee came to life. All at once he felt sure of himself. This was something he had rehearsed and he knew what to do. He found his voice.

"Here Wooster, come here boy," he called, and Wooster came slowly up, wagging his stub tail contentedly.

Tee Vee emptied a couple of cans of *Dogs Love It* into Wooster's pan and carried it over to the chalked circle on the floor. He didn't even worry about how he would look stooping or bending or squatting. He just reached down naturally and set the pan in the middle of the circle. He glanced at Wooster's position and noted that he was facing directly into Camera 2 so that the sponsor could see a really good shot of the beautiful dog gobbling up the beautiful dog food.

Tee Vee glanced at the monitor. The close-up shot already was on the air.

"Go to it Wooster boy!" Tee Vee shouted.

And nothing happened.

Wooster wagged his tail and looked up at Tee Vee and licked Tee Vee's face. He showed no interest at all in *Dogs Love It* dog food.

Wooster was so full of *Dogs Love It* dog food, from eating the four cans of the stuff dumped on the floor during rehearsal, that at the moment he was sure he never wanted to see another ounce of *Dogs Love It* dog food.

Tee Vee was becoming panicky. Nothing worse could happen on the *Dogs Love It Animal Shop* program than for a dog to refuse to eat *Dogs Love It*.

Tee Vee picked up the pan and held it under Wooster's nose. Wooster disdainfully turned his head away.

Tee Vee set the pan down, grabbed Wooster by the ears and shoved his nose into the pan. Wooster sprang back with a snarl and snapped at Tee Vee.

The ruin was complete. At long last, the shocked director recovered his wits, cut the picture off the air and substituted a picture of Mr. Gompton's horrified face.

This was one of those impossible situations. Mr. Gompton tried desperately to think of the right thing to say—something that would make the sponsor think he had never seen what he had just seen. Of course there was nothing just right he could say, so he said the wrong thing. He went right on spouting the regular commercial copy as if nothing had happened.

He could almost hear the viewers at home roaring with laughter and the sponsor at home groaning in rage. "All dogs love *Dogs Love It* dog food," Mr. Gompton's voice was saying. "You have just seen how my dog Wooster loves it. He can hardly wait till mealtime. And it's good for him. It will be good for your dog too. And your dog will like it just as much as Wooster does. Buy a can today."

Tee Vee had never felt so unhappy in his life. This was all his fault. He probably had lost Mr. Gompton his job and he had lost the show for Mr. Jules. Tears welled into his eyes. Poor Mr. Gompton, his face a deep crimson and his voice cracking, was still carrying on about how Wooster and all dogs love *Dogs Love It.*

Then Tee Vee made a decision to do something practically unknown in television. He decided to be honest.

He went right up to Mr. Gompton and through his tears he said:

"Mr. Gompton, it was all my fault. I know why Wooster wouldn't eat the *Dogs Love It* dog food."

Mr. Gompton stopped his spiel and stared at Tee Vee.

"Wooster was so full of *Dogs Love It* he just couldn't eat any more," Tee Vee hurried on. "I fed him four cans of it just before the show."

"You what?" shouted Mr. Gompton.

"Yes, sir," Tee Vee repeated. "I fed him four cans of it. I really didn't mean to, but Wooster and I were rehearsing and he pushed me over and spilled the dog food; then he pulled me over when Sharley bit his tail, and two more cans spilled, and both times Wooster ate all the *Dogs Love It* off the floor. Here, I'll show you the cans."

Tee Vee picked up the two cans he had just emptied and ran off-stage and picked up the other four, while Mr. Gompton just stared, unable to say a word.

He came back with six empty cans in his arms, and he faced straight into the camera and made a little speech to everybody watching.

"You can see the empty cans. *Dogs Love It* dog food is good dog food. But you can't blame Wooster for not wanting to eat *six* cans of it all at one time. He really does like it and that's why he ate every bite of those first four cans just a few minutes before we went on the air. So I hope you won't let my mistake keep you from buying *Dogs Love It* because the sponsor is very nice to let us put on this show and to pay for it, and he can't pay for it unless you buy *Dogs Love It* dog food. So I hope you will and I'm sorry for what I did and thank you."

Well, that did it. People with dogs went right out and bought whole cases of *Dogs Love It,* and some people without dogs went out and bought a few cans just because they felt sorry for Tee Vee when they saw

72]

his tears and because they thought he was so brave to be so honest.

The sponsor did not know at first whether to be angry or happy, but when all those orders for *Dogs Love It* started coming he knew which to be. He was so happy he sent Tee Vee a messenger with a gift. It was a whole case of *Dogs Love It* dog food, which Tee Vee didn't know what to do with, since he didn't have a dog. He tried to give it to Mr. Gompton, but Mr. Gompton already had a houseful.

And Mr. Jules, who had been watching the show on the set in his office, knew right away, as soon as Tee Vee made his speech to the audience, that this was going to sell more *Dogs Love It* than all the commercials in the preceding six months. He was mighty proud of the errand boy he had hired.

The rest of the show that night went fairly well. After Tee Vee had mentioned that Sharley had bitten Wooster's tail, Mr. Gompton noticed that Tee Vee had moved Sharley's chain. So he pretended that Sharley's chain was coming loose and managed to snap the chain back in its old place without anyone noticing. And sure enough, within a few minutes Sharley had reached the bag of groceries and toppled it over, making a most satisfactory mess of broken eggs and flour.

Only one thing went wrong. The lady guest who had brought in the monkey took her pet, a big rhesus, over to say hello to Sharley. Before Mr. Gompton could stop her, Sharley had taken a bite out of the big monkey's tail. Screaming with pain and rage, the big monkey leaped and landed on Mr. Gompton, and bit his hand.

Mr. Gompton finished the show with his hand behind his back because he did not want the blood to show and make children think pets are dangerous. As soon as the show was over a doctor was called and by the next day Mr. Gompton was in the hospital with a bad infection that nearly killed him. He recovered within a few weeks, but meantime who was to do *The Animal Shop* show?

Who else?

Who had sold more *Dogs Love It* dog food than anybody else? Who had the admiration of every viewer because he was so honest? Who was Mr. Jules so proud of?

Tee Vee Humphrey.

Mr. Jules called him into the office and told him that he and the sponsor had decided that the following week Tee Vee Humphrey should run *The Animal Shop* show all by himself.

M. C. TEE VEE

So it was decided that our young hero, Tee Vee Humphrey, would be M.C. (Master of Ceremonies) of *The Animal Shop* program the next week.

Of course there had to be a great deal of discussion before such an important decision could be made.

Mr. Gompton was still in the hospital and the doctor said he would be unable to return to the show for a month or so. Fay had the long-lasting, old-fashioned type of measles and it was certain she would be unable to return for a week or two.

Some people around the station thought one of the

announcers or an M.C. from one of the other shows should be substituted. But the director, Mr. Berry, said not to worry, that he could organize things so that Tee Vee really would not have too much to do. Besides, Mr. Jules had confidence in Tee Vee. The sponsor finally ended all discussion by insisting that Tee Vee do the program. He said that after that speech about Wooster and the dog food, Tee Vee had become a real *Dogs Love It* TV personality.

Tee Vee had plenty of help planning the next week's program. Mr. Jules, Mr. Berry, the stage manager, the cameramen, Mr. Betz, and even Miss Barns had lots of suggestions and wanted to help all they could.

The first problem was getting guests for the show, but this was not much of a problem. Mr. Gompton kept a big card file of all the pet owners who had written in, asking to be on the program. He had them all listed under "cat people," "dog people," "snake people," and the like.

Under "dog people" they found a man named Tom Gregg. The card read: "Bulldog. Interesting origin. Undershot jaw." Tee Vee did not know whether this meant that Mr. Gregg or the bulldog had an interesting origin and an undershot jaw, but either way, together, they should make a good pair of guests.

Under "snake people" they found a woman named Alvesta Shaffer. The card read: "Scarlet king. Looks like coral snake but ain't, thank goodness." Mr. Gompton probably could have explained more about what the notes on his cards meant, but he was too sick to care.

Mr. Jules's secretary called Mr. Gregg and Mrs. Shaffer and they were happy to come down for the show. For a third guest, Mr. Jules and Mr. Berry thought Tee Vee should play it safe and use Vernie Hoffman, who owned the real pet shop from which the TV program rented its "regular" animals each week. Mr. Hoffman had been on the show a number of times and he could come on first, to get Tee Vee started off right. They decided to let him bring and talk about any kind of pet he wished.

As the plans progressed (Tee Vee came to the station after school for conferences) Tee Vee became more and more excited. He also felt more and more important—too important. Mr. Jules noticed this and asked Tee Vee to stay in his office a few minutes after the Wednesday evening meeting.

"Look, Tee Vee," he said, when the others had gone. "Don't try to be a great actor—not yet. Just be a little boy on the show next Saturday. Mr. Berry has

[77

been directing that show for a long time. You will need him badly to take care of all the technical things. And he will—he will make it easier for you. Just forget about cameras and microphones and all that. The stage manager will send the guests in at the right time and signal them when to say good-bye and leave."

"Yes, sir," Tee Vee said.

"And, Tee Vee, remember that these guests of yours on the show will know all about their own pets. You won't have to tell *them;* your job is to get them to tell *you.* Ask questions, learn all you can."

Mr. Jules gave Tee Vee a pat on the shoulder and told him to hurry home to dinner. Tee Vee left, not feeling quite so important as he had. But he thought seriously about what Mr. Jules had said, and he spent every spare moment the next two days thinking up things he did not know but would like to know about bulldogs and snakes.

By show time, Tee Vee's mind was so full of questions he almost forgot to be nervous. Mr. Berry had arranged for an announcer to explain Mr. Gompton's misfortune and absence, and to say that Tee Vee was taking his place, before the camera ever came to Tee Vee. Mr. Berry had brought some grapes for Tee Vee to feed Sharley and that was what Tee Vee was doing when he was first seen on camera. He did not even know when he went on the air.

When the shop bell rang as the door opened, Tee Vee knew that his first guest, Mr. Hoffman, had arrived. Mr. Hoffman had decided to bring some golden hamsters with him. He told Tee Vee so many interesting things about the little mouselike but short-tailed pets that Tee Vee forgot all about the thousands of people watching them at home.

Since Mr. Hoffman was an "old-timer" on the show, Tee Vee knew he had no worries while Mr. Hoffman was there. This put him even more at ease. He just listened while Mr. Hoffman showed how tame the little hamsters were and explained how easy they were to care for. Mr. Hoffman said that all the millions of pet hamsters in Europe and America were the children and grandchildren of a single mother and her children dug from deep in their burrow in Syria, on the Mediterranean Sea, in 1930, and that the first ones did not reach America until 1938.

That seemed impossible to Tee Vee, but when he said so, Mr. Hoffman explained that a single pair of hamsters could have so many children and their children could have so many children until, at the end of only six months, there could be 200 hamsters from the single pair. If the 200 then produced as rapidly, there would be 20,000 by the end of another six months, two *million* in another six months, and so on. He warned that people with hamsters should be sure they did not escape. In the wild state they could multiply so fast they quickly could become a pest to farmers because of the grain they would eat.

Mr. Berry told the floor manager to signal Mr. Hoffman to leave, so Mr. Hoffman said he had to be going and then said good-bye to Tee Vee.

Tee Vee gave Sharley another grape, and then the shop bell rang again as Mr. Gregg entered with his bulldog.

Mr. Gregg was very friendly. He introduced himself to Tee Vee. He said he was very sorry to hear about Mr. Gompton being in the hospital, but that he knew Mr. Gompton's Animal Shop was in good hands. This made Tee Vee feel good. He patted the big bulldog that Mr. Gregg was leading on a leash.

"I'm so glad you came in," Tee Vee told Mr. Gregg. "I've been wanting to know how the bulldog got its name, and since you have one, maybe you can tell me. Is it because bulldogs have such wide and deep chests, like a bull?"

"Not exactly," Mr. Gregg replied, quite pleased

that Tee Vee had so gracefully started him off on his favorite subject. "See what a mild and good-natured pet my bulldog is. You petted him when we first came in, and he didn't even know you, so you can see what a friendly animal he is.

"But, I fear that his great, great, great, great, great grandfather was a bit more ferocious. Bulldogs originally were called bulldogs because they were used to attack bulls. Back when people were not as kind to animals as they are today it was considered good sport in England to have bulls and dogs fight as a sporting event. Bull-baiting, they called it. They also matched dogs against bears and the same kind of dog was best at both. I don't know why the best kind of dog was called a 'bulldog' instead of a 'beardog,' unless it was just more common to arrange fights with bulls than with bears."

Tee Vee was truly interested in what Mr. Gregg was saying and he listened intently. Mr. Berry took a close-up shot occasionally of Tee Vee's intense listening, which made viewers at home listen all the more intently too. Then Mr. Berry would go back with his cameras to Mr. Gregg's face, and after that, he would switch to a shot of Mr. Gregg's bulldog, Prince Gallant. Prince Gallant looked so powerful that you could imagine him fighting any bull, but, at the same time, so dignified and gentle that you knew he wouldn't do it. This was turning into an excellent television show without Tee Vee having to do anything except to act natural.

"The only chance the dog had against a bull was to grab the bull by the nostrils and try to hold his head down," Mr. Gregg continued. "The dogs that could do this best were the ones that could hang on best when the bull shook and tossed his head, trying to get the dog loose and catch him with his horns. The dogs that could hang on best were those with long lower jaws, with the teeth curved slightly backward. The harder the bull tossed his head, the harder this type of jaw hung on. So Englishmen who engaged in this dreadful sport selected dogs with undershot jaws, and that is how the breed we call bulldogs got started."

"Well, I'm glad these fine pets no longer have to fight bulls," Tee Vee commented with real feeling.

"Let me show you how that undershot jaw works," Mr. Gregg said, "without a bull." He held out a short stick for the dog to grab. As the bulldog's jaws clamped on it, Mr. Gregg lifted the stick until the dog was suspended in mid-air. Then Mr. Gregg started swinging the stick from side to side. The dog hung on with no apparent effort. Finally Mr. Gregg widened the swings and started twirling his own body so that he was swinging the dog all the way around at arm's length, and still the undershot jaw clung tightly to the stick. When Mr. Gregg slowed down, the dog's feet touched the floor and he regained his footing. Obviously he enjoyed this play. Even after he came to a standstill, he clung to the stick with feigned ferocity. He did not let go until Mr. Gregg gave a command.

Then Mr. Gregg (who had seen a signal from the floor manager) said he and his dog would have to be going.

Tee Vee wished they could stay longer, but he knew that the time was going by and that the show could run for only half an hour, so he thanked Mr. Gregg most sincerely, gave the gentle bulldog a friendly pat, and said good-bye.

It was time now for the commercial and Tee Vee called for Wooster. A stagehand had been keeping Wooster confined on a leash backstage, to prevent any possibility of trouble between him and the big bull-dog. Wooster came bounding out, hungry for his *Dogs Love It* dog food, and this time everything went smoothly. While Wooster attacked his food, Tee Vee explained again what had happened the week before. He pointed out that, as all could see, Wooster really did like the *Dogs Love It* dog food. So once more viewers went out to buy all the *Dogs Love It* dog food they thought their dogs could eat in the near future, and even the distant future.

After the commercial, the bell rang again and the snake woman, Mrs. Shaffer, came in with her pet scarlet king snake. She did not look at all like the snake woman Tee Vee had seen at a circus side show. She did not wear grass skirts or do a dance that made her wriggle all over. In fact she dressed just like Tee Vee's mother and looked something like her, which was not surprising, because she was a housewife just like Tee Vee's mother. The difference was that Mrs. Shaffer had become interested in snakes and kept them as pets.

"Do snakes *really* make good pets?" Tee Vee asked, as soon as he had introduced himself.

"Well," Mrs. Shaffer replied, "it depends on what you expect of a pet. Snakes are not affectionate like dogs or cats, but there are a lot of interesting things about snakes that I didn't know before I started keeping them."

"But aren't you afraid of them?" Tee Vee asked.

"Of course not," Mrs. Shaffer said indignantly, and indeed she was proving it. She was taking the scarlet king snake from its cage as she spoke and wrapping it around her neck. The snake seemed quite content and made no motion to bite.

Tee Vee had to admit that the little snake was beautifully colored. It had yellow and bright red bands around it, the colors separated by bands of black.

"What if it bit you?" Tee Vee asked.

"What if a cat scratched you?" Mrs. Shaffer asked back. "It would be about the same thing. This scarlet king and other nonpoisonous snakes have sharp but short little teeth and a bite is no more dangerous than a cat scratch. Not that they go around biting. Most of

[85

them won't bite you, even when first captured—certainly not after you have handled them awhile. Here, *you* handle Esther and see for yourself."

Tee Vee really hadn't planned to handle the snake at all. He had always heard that they were slimy and cold. But he had no choice. Mrs. Shaffer took Esther from around her neck and wrapped her around Tee Vee's neck, placing Tee Vee's hand around the snake's neck as she did so.

Tee Vee's first reaction was to jump and throw the snake from him. He didn't, because he thought that Mr. Gompton would not do such a thing, but the idea was so plain on his face that Mr. Berry in the control room watched the close-up shot of Tee Vee's face and the snake's head and said to nobody: "What a show. What a picture. What a TV show."

Much to his surprise, Tee Vee Vee noticed that the snake did not feel slimy at all. It did not even feel cold, really. Snakes are "cold-blooded," Mrs. Shaffer explained, which means that they assume the temperature of their surroundings. The snake was the same temperature as the temperature of the air in the studio.

Tee Vee took Esther from around his neck and placed her on the floor to see how she moved about

86]

without any feet. Esther just lay there, darting her tongue in and out, until Tee Vee let go of her neck and prodded her in the tail a little. She moved forward a few inches.

"Why does she dart her tongue in and out?" Tee Vee wanted to know. "Is she angry?"

"Snakes don't seem to see very well," Mrs. Shaffer told Tee Vee, "but they have a good sense of touch in their tongues. Darting the tongue in and out helps them when traveling. They can hear too, even though their ears are covered by a layer of outer skin and you can't see them. And snakes can feel heat so much better than we can that they can chase a rat in the dark, guided only by the heat they feel from the rat's body."

While Mrs. Shaffer was talking, Mr. Berry was having a fine time shooting a closeup of the snake on the floor, and of Tee Vee trying to get it to move more. Tee Vee gave Esther another gentle prod.

Then all at once Esther took off like a blue racer. Tee Vee grabbed for her, but too late. Esther darted under the shelving along one wall, with Tee Vee right after her as fast as hands and knees would take him. But by the time Tee Vee reached the spot and looked under the shelves, Esther was no longer there. She had disappeared.

[87

There was nothing very mysterious about this, because there were any number of cracks between the "flats" that made up the set, and under them, through which a small snake could have escaped from *The Animal Shop* set. The disappearance was not really mysterious, but it certainly was embarrassing.

The floor manager already was signaling Mrs. Shaffer that it was time she left. She had come in with a snake and she could not very well leave without one, as if she had forgotten her dear pet. Tee Vee could think

of nothing to do. It was his fault the snake had escaped, but he and Mrs. Shaffer could not go in back of the set looking for it just then. You can't leave three television cameras shooting an empty set while you go behind it looking for a pet snake.

But Mrs. Shaffer thought well and fast.

"Don't worry about Esther," she told Tee Vee. "She likes to hide that way, but she will make an appearance before you close up tonight. Just drop her off at my house on your way home."

Tee Vee gratefully said he would.

"I'd stay now and hunt for Esther," Mrs. Shaffer continued, conscious that the floor manager was pointing to his watch and making violent motions for her to get off-stage, "but I have to hurry home. Some guests are coming." Mrs. Shaffer expected no guests, but the excuse provided a graceful way to leave before Mr. Berry ran out of time and had to cut the show off the air without the regular closing. So Mrs. Shaffer left.

But where was Esther?

THE MISSING SNAKE

As soon as Mrs. Shaffer was out of *The Animal Shop's* door and had stepped into the make-believe street, which was just part of the studio, she dashed back behind the set to find Esther. She did not find Esther.

Even after *The Animal Shop* show was over and *The Animal Shop* set had been taken down and stored away, she did not find Esther. Tee Vee, Mr. Berry, those members of the crew who were not afraid of snakes, Mr. Hoffman, and even Mr. Gregg and his bulldog helped Mrs. Shaffer try to find Esther. They looked everywhere, or thought they had. But no Esther. Finally they had to give up.

Mrs. Shaffer, of course, was very sad at the loss of her snake, and Mr. Jules was very unhappy at having a snake, even a nonpoisonous one, loose somewhere in the building. Tee Vee's spring school vacation started that Saturday, and Mr. Jules offered him a job for the whole week if he would only look for the snake as he ran errands. Tee Vee, of course, was grateful for a chance to earn some extra money and extra experience. Besides, he was so excited about television he could think of no place he would rather spend his spring vacation than at WHAT.

So Tee Vee assured Mrs. Shaffer that he would keep a sharp eye out for Esther and would return her as soon as she was found. Tee Vee made the rounds of the whole building and begged everyone not to get excited and kill Esther in case she turned up unexpectedly, but to call him instead.

When Tee Vee got home that evening his mother and father were very complimentary about the job he had done as M.C. on the program. "There was so much interesting material on the show I could not have stopped watching if I had wanted to," his mother said. "You did everything just right," his father praised him. "Everything went very smoothly."

"What about the snake getting away?" Tee Vee asked. "That must have looked pretty bad."

"Oh, that was just cute," his mother said.

Tee Vee already had learned that a mistake that bothered people at the station a great deal often went unnoticed by viewers at home. Or at least the mistakes did not seem as important to viewers as they did at the studio. But it still was true that no one had mentioned anything to him about doing the following Saturday's show. Tee Vee hoped it was because there was so much excitement about the lost snake that Mr. Jules forgot to mention it. Or maybe Mr. Jules just assumed that Tee Vee knew he would M.C. the next show, since Mr. Gompton would not be back for a month or so yet.

But Tee Vee could not be sure, and when Billy Herman dropped by on Sunday afternoon, he became less sure.

"Well, so far as I could see," Billy said, "you just stood there listening. Anybody could do that. You don't have to be a great actor to do that."

Tee Vee tried to explain that he did what he was supposed to do. By asking questions at just the right

92]

time, he kept the guests talking about interesting things. And that was what the show was supposed to be. Nobody who watched *The Animal Shop* expected the M.C. to step to the center of the stage and start reciting Shakespeare.

"Well," Billy said, "you sure 'goofed' with that snake. Don't tell me you were supposed to let that snake get away."

Thus Tee Vee was not too happy when he reported for work the following Monday morning, the first day of his spring vacation. In the first place nobody had seen Esther. She might have escaped from the building, or she might be dead, or might be in the building and alive, but where? In the second place, Mr. Jules had gone on a trip over Sunday and would not be back until Monday afternoon. So Tee Vee still did not know whether his career as an M.C. was just beginning or already had ended.

Tee Vee searched the building again for Esther, without success. He was glad to have something to take his mind off his troubles when Mr. Betz asked him to help usher women to Studio C for the *Ladies, Stand Up!* program, which was on every weekday morning at 11 o'clock. After the last of the ladies, about 200 of them, were seated, Tee Vee reported back to Mr. Betz. But Mr. Betz had nothing for him to do for an hour or so. Tee Vee decided to join the ladies himself to kill time and see how Harry Manley, the M.C., handled the program.

The show ran a full hour and most of that time was taken up with Mr. Manley just talking, except for a little music and a few interviews with the visiting ladies. Mr. Manley had a great "gift of gab" and usually he had no trouble saying things that made the ladies giggle or snicker. But even to Tee Vee, as inexperienced as he was, it was obvious that today Mr. Manley was having trouble.

Maybe Mr. Manley had been up too late the night before, or had a stomach-ache, or something. At any rate he did not seem able to say anything that the ladies considered either funny or valuable. The 200 women just sat there with grim faces and stared at Mr. Manley. Tee Vee felt embarrassed for Mr. Manley and was glad he was not standing up there as M.C in his place.

Finally, in desperation, Mr. Manley told about the lost snake. Of course he and everybody else connected with the station knew about Esther, but the ladies did not. Mr. Manley felt he had to do something to arouse their interest. That is why he concluded with:

94]

"So Esther is still lost, presumably alive and hungry. She disappeared on *The Animal Shop* program, which comes from Studio B, just down the hall on this floor. She probably still is somewhere on this floor. For all I know, that snake might be in this very studio this very minute! It might come wriggling down the aisle right beside you, or be under your chairs!"

Well, that aroused interest, without doubt. Some woman screamed and then a lot of other ladies screamed and the *Ladies, Stand Up!* show had never better lived up to its name. The ladies stood up. Some climbed on chairs. Others started a rush toward the doors. Mr. Manley jumped up on his desk and screamed at the women to be calm. Tee Vee rushed to the door and tried to help stop the stampede. Finally, between Mr. Manley and Tee Vee, order was restored.

"I'm sorry, ladies," Mr. Manley apologized. "I didn't mean to get you excited. There is no snake here. I just said for all I knew, it *might* be here. Just for fun, you know—that's why I said it."

He noticed now that it was Tee Vee who had been helping at the door, so he decided to use Tee Vee to help clear himself with the ladies.

"I told you that the snake appeared last Saturday

[95

on *The Animal Shop* program. Well, by good luck, we have here in the studio right now the man, or boy rather, who M.C.'d that show Saturday, Tee Vee Humphrey. If he was not afraid of the snake, why should we be? Tee Vee, come up here and explain to my good friends that the snake is not poisonous."

Caught by surprise, Tee Vee blushed quite a bit, which the ladies thought charming, and went to the front of the studio.

"Mr. Manley is right," Tee Vee began. "There is nothing to fear from Esther. Until Saturday I did not know much about snakes, but Mrs. Shaffer, the woman who owns Esther, told me there are very few poisonous snakes in the entire United States. Probably the most dangerous is the small coral snake. It gives no warning, as a rattler does. And its venom acts on the nervous system, bringing about paralysis in a short time. It is brilliantly colored with yellow, red, and black rings encircling its body. Now the scarlet king . . ."

But Mr. Manley had noticed a movement on the floor beside him. As he looked closer an expression of horror spread over his face. It was a rather small snake and he noticed, just as Tee Vee was saying that the deadly coral snake has yellow, red, and black rings,

that the snake on the floor had yellow, red, and black rings.

"Heaven help us!" Mr. Manley shouted in a most unmanly fashion. "A coral snake!"

Poor Mr. Manley dived for the door and ran shouting down the hall and down the steps and out the front door.

Of course the ladies did not panic at all. They laughed and laughed. They had been fooled once and they did not intend to be fooled again. They thought Mr. Manley was very funny to try to scare them twice. Not even those in the front row saw the snake, because they had been looking at Tee Vee when it crawled across the floor, and now it was hidden by Mr. Manley's desk.

On his part, Tee Vee was almost as excited as Mr. Manley, but for quite different reasons. When Mr. Manley shouted, Tee Vee looked around and there was Esther! Tee Vee was so happy at finding the lost snake for Mrs. Shaffer, he forgot all about Mr. Manley and the ladies and television. He made a dive for Esther and caught her with one hand just behind her head. Then still on his knees behind the desk, he wrapped Esther around his neck just as Mrs. Shaffer had done.

Then he happily stood up.

That really did it. When the women actually saw the snake, and with Mr. Manley's shouts about a deadly coral snake still ringing in their ears, they really panicked. They rushed for the doors, which fortunately were double doors and so wide that no one was crushed. They streamed from the building and

no power on earth could have stopped them this time.

Tee Vee was left alone facing a camera with the red light burning in front, meaning he was on the air. The other camera had been knocked over in the rush. Tee Vee petted the snake with his free hand and said the snake was really completely harmless.

"What I was going to say when I was interrupted," he told the camera, "was that Mrs. Shaffer thought her pet very clever to look so much like a poisonous coral snake. Many of its enemies in nature might mistake this harmless little scarlet king for the poisonous coral and run in fear, just as Mr. Manley did. I didn't get to say that although both kinds of snakes have red, black and yellow bands, the order is different. On the coral snake the order is red, yellow, black, yellow, red —the black bands always bordered by yellow. You can see here on Esther that the order is red, black, yellow, black, red—the yellow bordered by black. It makes all the difference."

Tee Vee noticed the floor manager signaling that it was time for the show to close.

"So," he concluded, "thanks for watching this morning, and I am sure Mr. Manley will be back to welcome you again tomorrow morning."

Mr. Manley *was* back the next morning, though a

little shaken and *very* embarrassed. The story was all over the station and all over the community about how he had run from gentle little Esther.

For a long time his face turned as red as Esther's scarlet bands whenever anyone mentioned the word "coral" or "snake" or even "Esther" in his presence.

This was sad, Mr. Betz commented, because Mr. Manley's wife's name was Esther, and it is very difficult to live with a wife named Esther without hearing the name quite often.

Of course, as soon as he was off the air that Monday morning when Esther was found, Tee Vee took the snake home to Mrs. Shaffer, carrying her under his coat so she would not get chilled. Mrs. Shaffer was overjoyed to have her pet back, and Tee Vee's conscience quit bothering him about having been careless enough to let Esther escape in the first place.

Tee Vee stopped for lunch on the way back to the station, and when he got there Mr. Jules was back. Now he would know whether next Saturday he would be "M.C. Tee Vee" or just plain "Tee Vee."

HOW CURIOUS IS
A MONKEY

WHEN Mr. Jules returned, he called a meeting of Mr. Berry, Tee Vee, and the sponsor to decide about the next Saturday's *The Animal Shop* program.

Mr. Jules said things had gone very well since Mr. Gompton's illness, but in all honesty, much of what had happened turned out well just because of luck. He said he thought the next program should be very carefully planned and that there really should be something quite different on it. Did he mean they should try another M.C.?

"If you want something different on the next show," Tee Vee said quickly, "I have a suggestion. Instead of just having pet owners on the show as guests, why not have a scientist as a guest—a scientist who uses animals in his experiments?"

"That sounds good," Mr. Jules said, and Mr. Berry and the sponsor agreed. "But where can we get such a scientist?"

"That's why I thought of it," Tee Vee explained. "My uncle, on my father's side, is Professor Harlow Humphrey at the University of Wisconsin. He's a psychologist and he uses monkeys in his experiments. He says if he can learn all about a monkey's mind he may be able to learn more about humans. Right now Father says he is trying to find out whether monkeys really have a lot of curiosity. And he uses fancy machines in his experiments that might look good on television, if he could bring them and work them."

The sponsor insisted that Tee Vee telephone his uncle right then and there. The telephone connection went through quickly and Uncle Harlow said he would be happy to come. He said he would bring his machines and lots of monkeys because he would like the general public to know how his monkeys were being used in the interest of science.

Mr. Jules was so pleased that he suggested the entire show be devoted to Uncle Harlow. And, if Mr.

Jules had any doubts as to whether Tee Vee should
M.C. on the next show, this settled it. Professor
Humphrey was Tee Vee's own uncle, and certainly the
professor would be pleased to have his own nephew
as M.C.

Tee Vee then brought up a subject that had been
worrying him. Of course he wanted to continue doing
the show, at least until he could get some praise from
his friends at school. But should not Fay, Mr. Gompton's daughter, have a chance at it? She was Tee Vee's
age and she really had much more experience because
of helping her father on the show for so long.

Mr. Jules said he thought Tee Vee was very gen-
erous to make the suggestion, but that because of
Uncle Harlow, Tee Vee should be on the program.
However, Fay could be on too, if she wanted. He telephoned her. Fay said she had about the longest siege
of measles the doctor had ever seen and she really
thought she should stay in another week. But she said
to thank Tee Vee for being so thoughtful.

So all was arranged and the following Saturday *The
Animal Shop* had more monkeys in it than ever before
at one time. Uncle Harlow brought a dozen of the 50
or 60 he used in his work. They were in cages scat-

tered around the set, and most of the rest of the space was taken up with experimental devices.

Much to Tee Vee's surprise, Uncle Harlow, just before the show, seemed more nervous than his monkeys. He was accustomed to lecturing to college students, but there was something about television that made him very nervous. Remembering how frightened he had become on his first appearance on *The Animal Shop*, Tee Vee could sympathize.

When they went on the air, Tee Vee asked his uncle a couple of questions before they started experiments. He thought this would calm him and make him forget the cameras and it helped greatly.

First, Tee Vee asked his uncle why he used monkeys to study, when dogs or cats would be much cheaper and easier to obtain and raise.

"Because monkeys are much more intelligent," Uncle Harlow replied. "Dogs and cats really are quite stupid compared to monkeys."

Tee Vee hoped the *Dogs Love It* dog food sponsor would not be offended at this. He was a bit shocked himself.

"But dogs are *very* intelligent," he contended. "People write in to *The Animal Shop* and tell how their dogs are so smart they watch the program and get excited when another dog is shown on the television screen."

"A dog can recognize his image in a mirror, because the image is three-dimensional," Uncle Harlow admitted. "But there is no evidence that a dog can recognize a two-dimensional picture of a dog as a dog or anything else. The best they could do would be to see movement on the TV screen. They would not know it was a dog."

"Then why do they bark at a dog on the TV screen?" Tee Vee demanded.

"Because when there is a dog on the screen, there usually is a bark. A dog would recognize the bark as that of a dog, even if he could not recognize that the picture on the screen was a dog. No, dogs and cats are no more intelligent than racoons, pigeons, canaries, crows, starlings, or probably pigs, rats, and bears. A dog's only claim to intellectual fame is that he responds better to the spoken word than most other animals, and, also, he's a lot smarter than cows, horses, and elephants."

"Elephants!" Tee Vee said in surprise. "Why, I've always heard that elephants are so smart they never forget."

"It is true that elephants seldom forget," Uncle Harlow stated. "But that is because they are not smart enough to learn very much, so they don't have much to forget. I recall that when you were quite small, Tee Vee, you could recite the story of 'The Three Little Pigs' through, word for word, and that we all got tired of hearing you do it. I'll bet you could not do that now. Don't worry about it. That means your mind is better now, not worse. You are learning more now, so it is easier to forget more."

Tee Vee said he was anxious to see some experiments with the fancy machinery, but he wanted to know why such fancy equipment was needed. Why not just sit down in a chair and watch the monkeys in an ordinary cage?

"Well," said Uncle Harlow, "in science we have to *measure* things exactly, so we can make comparisons. But with monkeys there is another reason. Here, I'll let you prove it to yourself."

Uncle Harlow set up a big screen in front of one of the cages, so the monkey could see nothing but the screen. Then he gave the monkey a lock to try to unfasten, and placed a small mirror at one end of the screen.

"Now suppose you want to observe the monkey try

to solve that lock puzzle," he told Tee Vee, "and you do not want to disturb him. What would you do?"

"I would watch his reflection in that tiny mirror," said Tee Vee.

"Exactly. That's what we thought to start with. But try it."

Tee Vee moved his head until the angle was just right and he could see the reflection of the monkey.

"What do you see?" asked Uncle Harlow.

"The monkey looking at me!"

"That's just it. The monkey is so smart and so curious that he is just as anxious and able to spy on you, as you are to spy on him. He's watching you instead of working on the lock. Now you see why we had to devise special equipment. If we just want to observe him, we use a special kind of glass which passes light only one way. We can watch him through the glass, but he cannot see through the glass from his side to watch us."

"That certainly proves that monkeys are curious," Tee Vee commented.

"Yes, but it is not a precise measurement that I could report to other scientists. I have a machine here though, that proves *how* curious individual monkeys are. I have found that the more intelligent the animal is, the more curious he is. So if you know a boy who is very curious about everything, that probably means he is very intelligent."

Uncle Harlow demonstrated how the machine works. The device was a box with only one opening, a little door or window. It worked automatically and had a clock, cogs, gears, rods, and sliding screens. The monkey inside could push the door open every 30 seconds and peek out, if he were curious enough to do so. The door then closed automatically.

Uncle Harlow was afraid that the monkey would be too excited by the trip from the university and the strange surroundings of the studio to work the device. But he had Tee Vee flick on the switch.

Gears turned and rods moved and Tee Vee could hear a metal screen inside slide away from the door. Both Tee Vee and Uncle Harlow stared breathlessly at the wooden door, wondering whether the monkey inside were curious enough and not too frightened to push it open.

Almost instantly the door flew open as the monkey gave it a push, and there in the window was the face of a very curious monkey indeed. The monkey glanced at the lights and the cameras, then stared intently at Tee

Vee. Fascinated, Tee Vee stared right back and without realizing he was doing it, moved up to the little window. The monkey slowly retreated to the back of the box, never taking his eyes from Tee Vee's. Then the metal screen slid back into place, so that neither could see the other.

Uncle Harlow burst out laughing.

"Tee Vee," he said, "I don't know which we are testing, you or the monkey."

In 30 seconds the door popped open again.

"How long will he keep that up?" Tee Vee asked.

"We have had them keep at it for almost a whole day and night, never stopping, and without food or sleep. A monkey has to be very curious to do that. And, interestingly, we have found that the average monkey will keep at it longer to get peeks at a toy electric train, than to see a dish of peanuts, grapes, and meal worms. And to monkeys, peanuts, grapes, and meal worms are as delicious a combination as you would consider a chocolate milkshake, a hamburger with catsup, and potato chips. So you see curiosity is a very important thing in making monkeys do what they do, and the same is true of us."

Tee Vee, in listening to Uncle Harlow, had leaned

an elbow on the table which supported the monkey's box. This brought his head quite close to the window. Next time the door popped open, the monkey's hand shot out to give Tee Vee's ear a sharp tweak. Mr. Berry got a good close-up picture of Tee Vee's startled face, and the camera continued to watch as Tee Vee gave the monkey a dirty look and the monkey gave Tee Vee a

dirty look. Then the metal screen closed and Uncle Harlow said they had better move on to something else before a fight started.

The "something else" was a machine Uncle Harlow used to test the intelligence of the monkeys and find out how fast they could learn to solve problems. The strange-looking contraption included a cage with bars on one side so that the monkey could reach out. In front of the bars there was a sliding tray. Uncle Harlow pulled out the tray and as he did so, a solid screen slid down between the tray and the cage.

"Now," he pointed out to Tee Vee, "the monkey cannot see what I am doing. You will notice that there are little cups sunk in the tray. I will put a raisin in this cup and cover it with a square block. I will leave this other cup empty, but cover it with a round piece of wood. We want the monkey to learn that in this game the raisin is always under the square block."

"How can the monkey know, when he doesn't see you put the raisin under the block?" Tee Vee broke in.

"He can't know on the first try, but if he is intelligent, he will learn from experience."

The first time Uncle Harlow pushed the tray in and the screen raised, the monkey happened to pick the wrong block. But he remembered the mistake and after 'that he never missed. He always reached for the square block first, even when Uncle Harlow shifted the blocks from one side of the tray to the other.

Then Uncle Harlow played a trick on the monkey. He put the raisin under the round piece of wood. The monkey pushed aside the square block, as usual. No raisin! The monkey was furious. He screamed at Uncle Harlow and shook the bars of his cage in a great rage. But next time he pushed aside the round shape first, and there was the raisin.

Tee Vee wanted to know whether Uncle Harlow let the monkeys get very hungry before playing the game, so they would think harder to get the raisins. (No doubt he was remembering how Mr. Gompton cut down on Woostershire's food before the show to make sure he would gobble down *Dogs Love It* dog food with proper enthusiasm.)

"We do *not*," said Uncle Harlow with emphasis. "The monkeys play the game because they enjoy solving problems. They do just as well when they are too full of food to eat the raisins after they find them. And it is amazing what complicated games they can play. We have many tests, but let me show you just one more, if we have time."

Tee Vee glanced at the floor manager, who nodded his head "yes," so Tee Vee said there was time.

Uncle Harlow now placed five different shapes over five cups, and placed the raisin under a triangular-shaped block. Out at the side, he placed another triangular-shaped block.

"From playing the game before," Uncle Harlow explained, "the monkey knows that the block I place on the side is a clue as to which block the raisin is under."

He pushed in the tray and the screen went up. The monkey took one quick look at the triangular block at the side of the tray, immediately stretched out his arm, brushed the triangular block off the cup and claimed his raisin, on the first try.

Next Uncle Harlow covered five cups with blocks all the same shape and size, but different in color. He placed the raisin under a dark blue block, then he raised the screen and let the monkey, as a clue, see another dark blue block. Ignoring all the other colors, the monkey without hesitation knocked the dark blue block off the cup containing the raisin.

Tee Vee had no idea monkeys could learn such complicated things. He wondered how long it would take him to learn such a game, if he could neither hear nor read instructions.

"Do you punish them when they fail?" he asked.

"Never," said Uncle Harlow, "except that they don't get the raisins if they do it wrong. We find that they learn much more quickly if we keep them healthy and are kind to them. But some *kinds* of monkeys are smarter than others. I'll show you a kind that it's almost impossible to teach anything."

Uncle Harlow started for a cage at the far side of the set but he never got there. Sharley, the little squirrel monkey who was on the show every week, naturally curious being a monkey herself, had been watching quietly. Now, possibly because she was jealous or wanted to try the game herself, she suddenly started jumping up and down and screaming in her birdlike chirp.

This excited Uncle Harlow's monkeys. They forgot their lessons and screamed and growled back. And, since most of them were rhesus monkeys with deeper voices, they could make much more noise. Tee Vee and Uncle Harlow could neither hear each other talk nor quiet the monkeys.

Then one of the most hideous sounds ever heard in any jungle roared through the studio. It came from the cage toward which Uncle Harlow had started—for that cage contained a howler monkey.

What the howler monkey lacked in intelligence, it made up for in the unbelievable loudness and horror of its cry. Like all howlers, the monkey had a flexible bone in its throat which it expanded into a kind of hollow drum. Opening into the windpipe, this greatly magnified every sound the animal made, like a giant pipe organ. Its terrifying cries drowned out poor, squeaking little Sharley, and even the harsh cries of the rhesus monkeys.

At home, viewers jumped in their seats, and in the control room the sound engineer shouted that his equipment would be ruined. Mr. Berry ordered all the microphones turned off, so for a while viewers were treated to the sight of Tee Vee and Uncle Harlow running frantically around the set trying to quiet the monkeys—like characters in the old silent movies. There was no sound at all.

Then Mr. Berry shook his head and recovered his wits. He cut from the cameras on the set to the show's closing slides (which were projected from another room) and ordered the theme music played. The recorded theme music was played inside the soundproof control room, safe from the sounds of even howler monkeys. To kill the rest of the time, Mr. Berry stayed on the slide identifying the show and the one identifying the sponsor for a long time. Mr. Jules said later the program set a record for the longest closing in the history of the station.

But otherwise, he said, the show was "a *howling* success."

THE BIG DOG SHOW

TEE VEE's career as M.C. of *The Animal Shop* television program obviously was drawing to a close. In fact, he had one more week to go. Mr. Gompton, the doctor said, would be well enough to return after that.

Fay already was sufficiently recovered from her measles, but to Tee Vee's surprise she refused to take over the job of M.C. the following Saturday. She said she would help Tee Vee, if he wished, but she would not take the responsibility of being M.C.

There was a good reason for that, and when Tee Vee discovered what it was, he wished he could duck the responsibility too. He wanted to quit his job right then, but Mr. Jules said no, that was not the way a showman was supposed to act. He said they all wished Mr. Gompton could get back just that one week earlier, but he could not. So that was that and it was Tee Vee's responsibility as a showman and good employee to take Mr. Gompton's place this one more week.

The reason Tee Vee and Fay both were scared of that one show was that this was to be *the big show of the year.*

If Tee Vee failed on *the big show of the year,* how would the kids at school react then? It had been bad enough after the Uncle Harlow show. Led by Billy, Johnny, and Fred, the boys kidded him about not being a great actor at all. They said that with his uncle on the program, Tee Vee might as well have stayed home and watched—that he had not been needed at all. Tee Vee's mother told him the boys were just jealous and to ignore their kidding. But Tee Vee found it very hard to ignore it. He wished they would quit, and now he had an idea.

The three ringleaders all were in their last year of Cub Scouting and the Cubs were having a paper drive the following week to make money for the pack. Why not have Billy, Johnny, and Fred appear briefly on *The Animal Shop* program to ask people to get their old newspapers ready for the paper drive? If they all were "on the same team," so to speak, by being on television together, maybe they would cut out the kidding. Mr. Jules gave his consent and the three boys accepted the invitation with no urging at all. They jumped at the chance. Tee Vee decided maybe his mother had been right about there being some jealousy involved.

That settled, Tee Vee started worrying again about *the big show of the year.*

The reason this program was so important to the station and to the sponsor was that it occurred during the National Dog Show, and this year the National Dog Show was in the same city. Weeks before, the sponsor and station had decided to spend a lot of money to originate *The Animal Shop* program that week directly from the big auditorium where the dog show would be held. Arrangements already had been made with the National Dog Show people, and newspaper stories about the plans already had been printed. It was too late to back out, Mr. Gompton or no Mr. Gompton.

The judging would be completed just before the show. All the new national champions among all the breeds of dogs would appear on the show right after the judging—their first appearance on television. Doing the television show from the auditorium was the only way this could be done because the new champions still would be on display and could not be taken away to appear at the television studio downtown.

The sponsor thought this would be a wonderful thing for the program, but viewers were accustomed to seeing *The Animal Shop* set every week, with *Dogs Love It* dog food stacked on the counters and shelves and floor, and with signs on the wall. The sponsor did not want to lose this "sponsor identification," so he decided to move the whole set to the auditorium. The new champions and their owners then could come into *The Animal Shop,* which would be set up in a wide aisle, and the show would look the same as it did every week.

Of course it cost extra money to move the set from the studio to the auditorium and have it set up there. And it cost extra to move lights and microphones and cameras from the studio. It cost extra also to move the entire crew—the cameramen, the lighting men, the stagehands, the engineers, and the director—to the auditorium. And it cost extra to set up special equipment to "beam" the program by radio microwave from the auditorium to the studio so that it then could be sent out over the air to people's homes.

With all this extra money involved, the sponsor was very anxious for a good show. So was the station. And so was Tee Vee. Tee Vee suggested that this time the entire program should be rehearsed completely, just as if it were on the air, so that nothing, absolutely nothing, could go wrong. The sponsor and Mr. Jules agreed to this, even though this meant still more extra money for extra rehearsal time on camera.

During the week Tee Vee had lots of help making sure that all the people with dogs entered in the show knew about the plans. Everyone was alerted. Nothing must go wrong. Every exhibitor knew that if his dog were judged the champion in his class, he should take his dog to *The Animal Shop* set, at the intersection of Aisles 1 and 4, and have him there at exactly 1:15 P.M.

Meanwhile Tee Vee studied very hard about the different breeds of dogs and about how dog shows are run and how the judging is done, so he could ask intelligent questions about all the champions.

On the day of the show the set was moved to the auditorium hours ahead of time. The lights were set up and tests were made to make sure that the system of transmitting the sound and pictures to the station was working perfectly. As usually happens on such occasions, nothing seemed to work right at first, but, as sometimes happens, after a while, everything did.

Tee Vee was there early too. So was Fay, but she made it clear that she wanted to have very little to do with the show. If anything went wrong, she admitted, she would just as soon have it be Tee Vee's fault. He did not have to live with her father.

The auditorium was so huge and there were so many hundreds of dogs on exhibit that Tee Vee could not help feeling frightened. Thousands of people were there to see the dogs and see the judging. And, of course, the sight of *The Animal Shop* set up at the intersection of Aisles 1 and 4, the tops of the walls soaring high above the people and the dog cages, attracted a lot of attention too. After all, it is not often that one sees a pet shop, complete with walls, doors, counters, lights, and shelves loaded with dog food, set up right in the middle of an aisle at a dog show.

By 1 o'clock there were so many people crowded around *The Animal Shop* set that the cameramen had trouble moving their cameras about. The building manager had to set up a rope barrier to keep the peo-

[123

ple back far enough for the WHAT crew to do its work. It really was quite exciting.

The new "best of breed" champions, with their owners, all showed up at 1:15 as scheduled. There was plenty of time to do a complete rehearsal before the show. Tee Vee thought he never had seen so many beautiful, proud dogs. They looked and acted as if they knew very well that they had just earned blue ribbons. And, of course, the owners looked as proud as their dogs.

In fact, Tee Vee reflected, they *looked* a little like their dogs. The blue-ribbon poodle was owned by a fluffy, well-groomed woman who obviously was just out of the beauty shop herself. The boxer was owned by a muscular broad-shouldered man who looked as athletic as his dog. Tee Vee wondered whether owners unconsciously select dogs that are somewhat like themselves.

But there was work to be done, and Tee Vee turned his mind to his rehearsal. Tee Vee wanted this show to be perfect. There were so many champions he could not give much time to each dog, but he explained that to the owners. He told everyone just where to stand while waiting to go on the show, how to come through the door, and how to leave. Everyone was assigned an order for entering the set, so there would be no traffic jams. Tee Vee saved for the last the "best of show" dog, a Dalmatian that had won out in the judging over all the champions of all breeds.

The rehearsal was done just the way Tee Vee wanted the show to be on the air, and everything went very smoothly. Tee Vee would greet an owner, then have him set his dog on the counter and have him pose the dog just the way he had for the judges, and then tell something about the dog's good points that helped win the blue ribbon. Then Tee Vee would pet the dog and thank the owner, and tell him good-bye.

There were so many dogs he had to have several of them come in at the same time, to keep from using too much time, but other than that, everything was just as Tee Vee wanted it. He felt very good about the rehearsal and was glad he had suggested it. He no longer felt worried about the show, because everything that could be done to make sure it would be good had been done.

Well, not *everything*. There was one disastrous omission. And several people could share the blame because nobody, not even Mr. Berry, thought of it.

What happened—or rather what didn't happen— was that no one thought to tell the dog owners that this merely was a rehearsal and not the real thing.

It really is not surprising that they thought they were on the air when they went through the rehearsal.

126]

After all, the cameras were being operated and the red lights on them were flashing on and off as Mr. Berry called for the shots he planned to use on the air. There was a picture on the monitor screen at the side of the stage, in plain view of everyone.

They saw the floor manager with his stop watch, worrying about the time. They heard Tee Vee give the commercials. (You may be sure Tee Vee gave Wooster very little *Dogs Love It* dog food at the rehearsal!) They heard the announcer say good-bye at the end of the show and ask all the viewers to tune in again next week at the same time. This was all part of the rehearsal, but how were the dog owners to know? Every one of them, to a man (and to a woman too), thought he really had been on television and hoped his friends had seen him.

When rehearsal was over, Tee Vee went to the water cooler for a drink before the show, and when he came back *all* of his guests were gone!

Mr. Berry discovered the tragedy at the same time. It was only 30 seconds until air time. It seemed just too late to do anything. The blue-ribbon dogs had been returned to their cages and now were scattered all over the immense building. And goodness knew where all the owners themselves were by now. Obviously it would have taken at least an hour to round them all up again.

But time waits for no man, including television performers.

"We just can't go on," Mr. Berry said with trembling voice. "Oh, why didn't we foresee that this might happen, and tell them that was only a rehearsal. If I had just thought to tell them to stay. I'll have to call the station and tell them to fill the time with a film or something."

Tee Vee thought of all the money that had been spent to do the program from the dog show, and how much more Mr. Jules would have to pay to the sponsor if the show did not go on the air. He felt terrible; he felt worse than terrible. He felt worse than he had ever felt before in his whole life.

"We *have* to go on," Tee Vee said. "We just *have* to."

"Yeah, but with what?" Mr. Berry snapped impatiently.

It was only 15 seconds now until air time.

A MATTER OF LUCK

"WITH *what?*" Mr. Berry repeated bitterly. "If we go on, what do we go on *with?*"

"With *dogs,*" Tee Vee said desperately.

"*What* dogs?"

"*Any* dogs. Some of these people walking around the aisles are leading dogs. Go open the show!"

Tee Vee shouted at his pals, Billy, Johnny, and Fred who were standing by to go on the program and announce the Cub Scout paper drive.

"You three get out in the aisles and get dogs. Get anybody leading a dog—*any dog.*"

"I'll help too," Fay volunteered and the four youngsters dashed off.

"That's the worst idea I ever heard," Mr. Berry informed Tee Vee. "But I'll go along with it. We can't be any worse off than we already are. We'll both get fired either way."

Tee Vee took his place on the set. Mr. Berry ran for the portable control booth and started barking orders. He motioned frantically to the floor manager and gave him new instructions while calling for slides and music. The floor manager ran for the back of the set as the theme music started, and the first slide appeared on viewers' screens.

Fay grabbed the first person she saw who was leading a dog, and practically pulled owner and dog to the back of the set. The floor manager took over from there, while Fay dashed back into the crowd to look for another dog. By this time Tee Vee was ready for his first guest. The floor manager had no time to explain.

"You are on television," he stage-whispered to the bewildered old lady and pushed her and her dog through the door.

Before the startled woman had time to back out the door, Tee Vee ran over and took her by the hand.

"I'm *so* glad you dropped in," Tee Vee said, and you can believe he really meant it.

"I'm Tee Vee Humphrey," Tee Vee continued politely, "and your name please?"

"Mrs. Murphy."

"And this is your dog. What's his name?"

"Rover."

"Let's put him right up here on the counter," Tee Vee talked on. "Come on Rover, old boy. What kind is he, Mrs. Murphy?"

"Just plain dog," Mrs. Murphy replied.

Tee Vee had been so tense, even though he appeared quite at ease on the television screen, that he had not really taken a good look at Rover. Now that he did, he shuddered. Rover clearly was out of place at the dog show. He was, indeed, "just plain dog"—a mixture of three or four breeds that defied identification. He was a dirty gray with straggly medium-length hair. One ear was tattered, due to an honorable injury suffered long before in a dog fight. He looked a little like old Mrs. Murphy. Mrs. Murphy did not seem to belong at the dog show either.

"Did you enter Rover in the dog show?" Tee Vee asked without thinking, and bit his lip the moment the question was out of his mouth. No one would have entered Rover in the National Dog Show or any other show.

"No indeed," said Mrs. Murphy. "I just brought him down to see how the other half lives. All those fancy dogs! My goodness, the way these people baby them. Many a human baby gets less care than those fancy blue-blood dogs get, I'll wager you that."

"What are Rover's good points?" Tee Vee automatically asked. He could not see that Rover had *any* good points. It was a question he had intended to ask the owners of the champions, but neither they nor the champions were there, and he could think of nothing else to say.

"My Rover has two good points," Mrs. Murphy declared, not at all abashed. "He has a friendly eye and a friendly tail."

Indeed, as Tee Vee took another look at Rover, these *were* two good points. The little dog's eyes sparkled with friendship and his tail was beating a constant friendly tattoo on the counter top. Mrs. Murphy could not have given you the name of Rover's father or mother, and she certainly had no blue ribbons at home, but she did have a friendly, good-natured dog, and the more Tee Vee looked at the disheveled Rover, the more appealing he looked.

"I see what you mean," said Tee Vee. "Maybe Rover could never win any ribbons, but he's a good dog all

the same. I can see that you love him and he loves you."

"He loves the whole world," said Mrs. Murphy, with a wide sweep of her hand. "He's a fine, faithful

animal and you can't beat that, ribbons or no ribbons."

Taking a chance, Tee Vee asked whether Mrs. Murphy ever fed Rover any *Dogs Love It* dog food, his sponsor's product. If Mrs. Murphy had said no, Tee

[135

Vee did not know just what he would have said. But as luck would have it, Mrs. Murphy fed Rover *Dogs Love It* dog food all the time.

"Listen," Mrs. Murphy said, "like me, there's nothing fancy about Rover. But like me, he likes a good meal as much as the next one. And I see to it that he gets the best—*Dogs Love It* dog food."

Tee Vee was so relieved that he gave Mrs. Murphy a couple of cans of the dog food to take home, and they said good-bye with smiles all around and with Rover wagging his tail furiously.

By this time Billy had arrived in back of the set with another dog and owner in tow, and the stage manager sent them through the door.

This guest was a man with a chow that had been entered in the show but had won nothing. Tee Vee thought and said that the chow was a very beautiful dog whether he had won anything or not.

And thus it went for the whole show. The four friends kept dragging in guests and Tee Vee interviewed them. About half the guests the floor manager shoved through the door had entered their dogs in the show but had won nothing. The rest, like Mrs. Murphy, had come out just to look, and had dogs no one would consider entering in a dog show.

136]

There was not a champion or ribbon winner in the whole lot of them. They all were just "plain dogs" or pure-breds not quite good enough to win.

As the half-hour drew close to its end, the floor manager told Fay and the three boys they had gathered enough guests. Tee Vee was so worried he almost forgot that he had told Billy, Johnny, and Fred that they would be on the show. Just in time to get them on, he pretended he saw them pass the window and called to them to come in. Each boy made the brief little speech he had carefully prepared. They were so excited and frightened at being on television that each stumbled over a word or two and blushed when they did, but all in all, they got by very well.

The instant the show was over, a tear started down Tee Vee's cheek and he ran for the exit. Startled, his three pals ran after him and caught him as he was going down the auditorium steps.

"What's the matter?" Billy demanded.

"I shouldn't have done it," Tee Vee sobbed. "I should have kept still and let them put on a film, like Mr. Berry said."

"But you put *The Animal Shop* on the air when it looked impossible!" Fred practically shouted at Tee Vee. "You were great!"

"That was really using your head," Johnny joined in. "You used your head more than any great actor ever had to."

"And besides," Billy admitted, "I have decided just M.C.ing that show is not easy even when things go right. I was scared to death when I stood up there in front of those cameras, just to say a couple of lines."

"Yeah, that's right, Tee Vee," Johnny said. "We think a lot differently about it now. In my speech I forgot three words, mispronounced two others, and said one twice."

"Thanks, fellows," Tee Vee said. "I know you are trying to make me feel good, and I appreciate it." And another tear escaped one of Tee Vee's eyes. He turned dejectedly toward home. His three pals fell in with him.

"What's wrong then, Tee Vee?" Billy wanted to know. "What we told you was the truth. We weren't just trying to make you feel good."

"What's the sponsor going to think?" Tee Vee asked. "What *can* he think? He spent all that money for that special show and I did not have a single championship dog on the show. He spent all that money for nothing. I don't care about me. It was my last week

138]

anyhow. But Mr. Berry will get fired, just like he said he would."

"Aw, maybe not," Billy said, but he was not very convincing, because he thought maybe Tee Vee was right.

"And the sponsor will cancel the show," Tee Vee went on sadly. "Think what that will mean. Fay won't be on the show again, and she was so good to help get the dogs today. And her father will lose his job. And Mr. Jules will lose the income from selling time for the show. And they all have been so good to me. Now look what I've done to them."

"Well, it wasn't your fault," was the best Billy could manage.

"Yes it was," Tee Vee said. "If I had told people that rehearsal was just a rehearsal, everything would have been all right. Or, after that happened, I should have kept still and let Mr. Berry decide what to do."

By now they had reached Tee Vee's house. The three boys went in with him.

Tee Vee's mother tried to comfort Tee Vee too, but she had to tell him that Mr. Jules had called and said that the sponsor wanted to see Tee Vee at the hotel where he lived. It was so serious that he wanted Tee Vee's mother and father to come too. And the sponsor also wanted the three boys that "somehow" had gotten on the program that afternoon.

"Well, here it comes," Tee Vee said. "But it's okay. I deserve it."

But he said his three pals did not deserve it. Tee Vee had supposed that Mr. Jules had checked with the sponsor about his request to use Billy, Johnny, and Fred on the program. If there were any trouble about *that* it certainly was not their fault.

But the boys said that if Tee Vee was going to "get it," they wanted to be right there by his side. And if the sponsor wanted to make anything out of Tee Vee putting the show on the air without any champions, they said they had a few things they would like to tell him.

The meeting was three hours away, and it was a long wait. Finally the dejected group made their way to the sponsor's hotel. Mr. Humphrey started to telephone the sponsor's room from the lobby to say they had arrived, but Mr. Jules appeared. With solemn face he motioned them up a short stairway to the mezzanine and down a short hall. He stopped at a door and opened it.

"Go on in, please," he said.

As Tee Vee stepped through the door, he thought

140]

at first Mr. Jules had made a mistake. It was a large private dining room filled with people seated at tables. But as soon as Tee Vee appeared everyone jumped and chanted:

"TEE-vee, HUM-phrey; TEE-vee, HUM-phrey," and gave three cheers.

Then Tee Vee started recognizing people. These were the people from station WHAT—Lucille, the nice receptionist; Mr. Betz, Mr. Berry, Mr. Manley (and his wife Esther), Fay, and most of the dozens of other people Tee Vee had learned to know as errand boy—the accountants, the engineers, the cameramen, the carpenters, the announcers, and most of the rest. Tee Vee noticed too Mr. Gregg, the bulldog owner; Mrs. Shaffer, the owner of the other Esther (the snake), and other guests who had been on the show when he was M.C.

At a long, raised table on one side of the room Tee Vee recognized the sponsor and that is where Mr. Jules led Tee Vee, his mother and father, and his three pals.

"It's the best we could do on such short notice," the sponsor said as they were being seated. "But we were able to reach most of your friends. And they are all here to honor you."

"But aren't you mad about the show this after-

[141

noon?" Tee Vee asked, wondering whether he might be dreaming.

"Of course not!" the sponsor almost shouted. "Haven't you heard? Our company and the station have had the switchboards jammed ever since the show. The calls are from the thousands and thousands of people who *don't* own champions—and there are a lot more of them than winners. They couldn't get over it—the fact that you telecast the show from the auditorium where the National Dog Show was held and did not show a single winner, just beautiful losers and lovable curs. They loved it. And Tee Vee, my boy, those dogs they own eat a lot more *Dogs Love It* dog food than the handful of winners. So why should I be mad? I'm delighted!"

"But it was an accident," Tee Vee whispered honestly.

"I know all about it," the sponsor said. "Mr. Berry told me everything. It was an accident the champions were not on, but it was no accident the show went on the air, anyway. *You* did that. Now enjoy your food, and then we have a little surprise or two for you."

"Was it all right, about my three schoolmates being on?"

"Oh, sure," the sponsor said. "I approved that be-

142]

fore the show. I just thought you might like to have your pals with you on a happy occasion like this."

Well, after the dessert, Mr. Jules got up and told how he had happened to hire Tee Vee in the first place, and said he was the best errand boy the station had ever had.

"By chance," he concluded, "he also has acquired a little experience, perhaps not as the great actor he wished to become, but at least as a performer. I am sure he is not aware of it, since he was working to gain experience and for the fun of it, but there are certain union regulations concerning the minimum fees that must be paid performers. I have figured this out and I am happy to present you, Tee Vee, in addition to your $3 a week as errand boy, this check for your services on *The Animal Shop*. It is in the amount of $316.78! I hope you will put it away to help with your future education."

Then Fay rolled in a new bicycle, a lightweight racer with two-wheel brakes and lights powered by its own generator. She read a note from her father, Mr. Gompton, thanking Tee Vee for his help and hoping Tee Vee would accept the bicycle "as a token of appreciation."

Then the sponsor stood up and announced that he

had arranged for a two-week's vacation for Tee Vee, and his mother and father too, to Florida, all expenses paid.

"Now," he said, "I'm sure you all want to hear a word from Tee Vee Humphrey himself."

Tee Vee got up, embarrassed by it all, but extremely grateful. His voice was husky with emotion.

"Thanks to you all," he said. "I can't thank you

enough. You know as well as I do how unbelievably lucky I was in all the things that have happened— even my worst mistakes turned out well. But at the same time I did learn a lot. And the most important thing I learned was how much I still have to learn."

There was loud applause and the loudest came from Billy, Johnny, and Fred.

"There's just one more thing," Tee Vee concluded. "Mr. Jules, now that I no longer am an M.C., do I still have my job as errand boy? I'd like very much to continue that."

Mr. Jules just smiled happily and nodded his head.

A NOTE ON THE TYPE

THE TEXT of this book has been set on the Linotype in Baskerville. Linotype Baskerville is a facsimile recutting of a type face originally designed by John Baskerville (1706–75). Baskerville, who was a writing master in Birmingham, England, began experimenting about 1750 with type design and punch cutting. His first book, set throughout in his new types, was a Virgil in royal quarto, published in 1757, and it was followed by other famous editions from his press. Baskerville's types, which are distinctive and elegant in design, were a forerunner of what we know today as the "modern" group of type faces.

THE BOOK was composed, printed, and bound by H. Wolff, New York. Paper manufactured by P. H. Glatfelter Co., Spring Grove, Pa. Typography by Charles Farrell.